A
New Jersey
LOVE STORY
HEIRS TO THE THRONE

A NOVEL BY

MYIESHA MASON

JOIN MAJOR KEY!

To submit a manuscript for our review, email us at
submissions@majorkeypublishing.com

PROLOGUE

Camilla

*T*he saying goes that those women who are blessed to be mothers should take their responsibilities seriously. A mother's role is to love, nurture, and protect their children. No one or nothing should come between a mother and her child.

The role of a wife is to love, honor, and respect her husband. Although Troy and my vows weren't the traditional vows that a husband and wife take at an altar, they still meant the same. No one should come between a wife and her husband. We ride together, we die together, but what happens when one is forced to choose between her child and her husband? This was my current dilemma.

I stood in my living room with a gun in my hand and one pushed into my back. In front of me kneeled my husband and my son, Malachi.

"You choose, or I choose."

I was given the ultimatum to choose whether to shoot my husband or shoot my child. I'd never been faced with a decision that was so hard.

"Choose now, or I'll take them both out!"

1

"I can't choose. Please, just let them go, and kill me," I pleaded.

"Nope. Fine... if you can't choose, then I'll choose. Which one should I kill first? Enny, meeny, miny."

This person counted off with the gun pointing back and forth between Troy and Malachi.

"Okay, okay. I'll choose, please, let me do it," I interrupted.

"Fine."

I looked between the two of the three most important men in my life. They both looked back at me. Even as I held their lives in my hand, neither one of my boys showed fear... just strength and power. I married a king, and I raised a young king. Even in a situation that had my face flooded with tears, I stood proud of the both of them.

"I love you two so much."

"It's alright, sunshine. You do what you got to do. You save our boy," Troy ordered with a stern look in his eyes.

"No, Ma. Look at me," Malachi called, getting my attention. I looked over at him.

"You and dad have an epic love story. Something like that can't be replaced, but I can. You two are role models for Ruby, Mega, and I. You and dad's jobs are not finished yet. Your story does not end here. You choose me. You hear me?"

"Malachi, you shut the hell up. Camilla... baby, look at your husband, baby. I'm your target. Now pull the god damn trigger."

"Both you niggas shut the fuck up. Camilla, you have thirty seconds to choose, or I'm choosing."

I stood there, listening to the both of them beg me to shoot them and spare the other. My heart had never been so torn. What kind of sick bastard would put someone in this kind of situation? After all that Troy and I had done for him, this was how he repaid us. I knew something was wrong with him when we first took him in. He was a coward just like his father and grandfather.

"Ten, nine, eight—" he counted.

"I'm sorry, baby," I cried as I aimed my gun at my loved one. I closed my eyes and placed my finger on the trigger.

Pow!

MALACHI

Hook: (Bryce & Nico)
"We young'n we reckless, cock back and leave another
   nigga breathless.
We young'n we reckless, I'm eating ya mama rent money
   for breakfast.
We young'n we reckless, whole family run down and
   leave yo' ass neckless.
Been running this game since the eighth grade, the
   hustle in me was homemade. Product of an
   involuntary drug trade, mama was a thug popped one
   in that bum nigga eye shade. Born from a queen at
   the age of fifteen. Never knew my pops but my step
   pops stepped up. Showed me how to be a real nigga,
   no homo but I love you, nigga."

*N*ico rapped his verse as we all stood, rapping along. He
and Bryce had a show at Bliss Lounge, so the whole
family had come out to support. These two had dreams of becoming
rappers, and today, they were finally getting their chance. I couldn't be

3

any prouder of my little cousins, especially Nico. He had come a long way from trying to be a dope boy to now focusing on things more positive.

"GO, BABIES!" Auntie B yelled as Bryce started rapping his verse. My aunt Blaize was a trip, but you couldn't help but to adore everything about her. Her and my aunt Tiff were sisters, and the crazy part was that they were raised apart and both had rocky pasts. Aunt Tiffany, who was Jace and Nico's mother, was traded by her mother for crack when she was a teenager. That was the inspiration behind Nico's lyrics. Aunt Blaize was a victim of domestic abuse, in which my uncle Knight, who was a detective then, had rescued her. Aunt Blaize called him her knight in chrome armor, and I could see why. They had been through so much in the past, but they still managed to stay together and get through it.

I'm not sure if their story could compete with what my dad and my mom had been through. Now those two were a different story. They'd been through hell and back. My mother had a few bodies under her belt over my father. My mother was crazy, and I don't mean that lightly. Maybe insane was more appropriate for my mother. She had more guns than a nigga could count and a collection of machetes that she kept on the wall of the garage. My mother could be scary at times. I think my father was even scared of her. To be honest, I'm shocked they were even here tonight. The two of them didn't really socialize unless it was a family event or my little brother, Mega, had a football game.

"Heyyyy, are we late? What did we miss!" Pryce yelled as she and Lil' Ruby came in the VIP section we had booked for the night. My lil' sister, Ruby, came over and gave me a hug and a kiss. My sister was my motherfucking baby, for real. I would kill for her and my mom. I was protective over them. So many people often mistook me as Ruby's father and my mom's husband.

"Why y'all late?"

"Chill, sis," Ruby answered.

"Yeah, aight. Don't get f'd up, little girl," I spoke, censoring myself because my mom was here.

"Malachi, you are not my father. You may look like him, but I did not come from ya ball sac, now did I?"

"Aye, little girl, watch ya mouth. I don't give a shit if you're eighteen.

I'll still beat that ass," my father said to Ruby. She stuck her tongue out and continued rapping and dancing to the music.

My sister had just turned eighteen and was due to graduate in a few weeks. To say we were all shocked to hear that her ass would be graduating was an understatement. No, she wasn't dumb. She was actually pretty fucking smart. At sixteen, she was helping me with my college homework, and at times, my father would sit her down and have her balancing the books from the club and my mother's daycares. We were shocked because Ruby's ass was forever acting out in school. She'd been suspended several times, and they had threatened to expel her. My parents had been called to the school so many times, you would have thought they were school staff.

The teachers hated my sister because she was so fucking smart that she was often challenging what they were teaching. One day, the teacher got so mad that she told Ruby if she thought she was so smart, then she should get up and teach the class. Being the smart ass she was, Ruby got up and started teaching the class. She was later kicked out for being noncompliant. Personally, I thought they were pushing my sister out of high school. They just wanted to get rid of her little ass for good.

My mother applied for a few colleges for Ruby, and after they saw Ruby's perfect 4.0 GPA, she was being offered full scholarships to over eight colleges. She swore up and down that she wasn't going to college, but that would be over my mother's dead ass body.

"Ayyyee, that's my brother!" Pryce yelled as she danced to her brother's rap. She was the angel of the family… like literally. In a few days, she was headed to another country to do missionary work with one of the churches she volunteered at. My aunt Blaize wasn't too thrilled about her baby girl going to a foreign country, but after some convincing from Unc, she changed her mind and let her go. It was only for three weeks. Her parents were throwing her a going away party tomorrow, being that she was leaving first thing Sunday morning.

After Nico and Bryce were done performing, we all sat outside and waited for them to come out. The partygoers started to file out of the club, being loud and rowdy. I spotted Bryce and Nico come out of the club, followed by their little entourage.

"There they go right there," I mentioned to everyone, getting their attention.

"Yurp!" Ruby's ghetto ass called after deciding to stand her little ass on the top of my hood. She was lucky I loved her little ass, or I would have knee checked her ass real quick. The rest of the family started cheering them on as the two of them came walking over by us.

"You guys did so good," Aunt Tiffany cheered as she embraced them one by one, and the whole family followed. We were a very loving and supporting family. Nothing and no one came before family. That was our motto.

The sound of a four-wheeler coming in our direction caught my attention. I knew it couldn't be anybody but Jace's dare devil ass. He, followed by his bike crew, came speeding in our direction and started doing tricks in the middle of the parking lot.

Jace had been riding motorcycles since he was seventeen. Uncle Swift bought him his first four-wheeler on his sixteenth birthday which pissed Aunt Tiffany off. She was very overprotective of her kids. She needed to know where they were at all times. She couldn't deal with the fact that the boys were grown as hell. Neither one of them lived with her. Nico lived with his baby mother, and Jace was renting to own a house out in Garfield, New Jersey.

Jace made his money boosting luxury cars. They would give him a list of the makes, models, and colors of cars, and he had to bring them the exact cars. According to him, he made at least five grand a car, and if it was a top luxury car like an Ashton Martin or something, he was paid close to ten grand.

Jace and I were the closest out of everyone. He was older than I was by two years. Before I decided to go to college, he tried to get me a job boosting, but I wasn't about that life. Besides, I had no reason to steal. My parents kept my siblings and I wanting for nothing. Swift did the same with Jace and Nico. He kept their pockets full, but Jace wanted to start making his own money, so he didn't have to depend on his stepfather for anything. Nico, on the other hand, was so set on becoming a rapper that he wasn't really trying to do anything else with his life. Nico was determined to make it in the rap game by any means necessary.

Jace's little biker act drew a lot of attention which got the attention of all the party goers. They all started making their way to where we were.

"Oh boy... it would take my son to make a scene and get everyone's attention."

"Come on, Ma. You know I does this. I'm a celebrity in these streets," Jace responded as he hopped off his bike and embraced his mother.

"I know you're a hood star, you hood booger. You missed your brother's show."

"Yeah, I know, but I had some business to attend to. I already know lil' bro smashed it like always," he affirmed, walking up to Nico and giving him a brotherly hug.

"You already know I smurdered the show. Nah mean?"

"I know. I taught you everything you know."

"Whatever, nigga," Nico spat as they started tussling. Although Nico was the youngest brother, he outgrew Jace by at least four inches. They were both popular with the ladies. I was shocked that they both didn't have boat loads of kids in these streets.

"Cuzzo, what's good with you? How's my god baby?" Jace asked, jumping on the hood of someone's car.

"She's good. I spoke to her earlier," I answered, referring to my daughter, Mya, who was staying out in Minnesota with her mother. She was two years old, and I hated to say it, but she was a mistake. Her mom and I were at a teacher's workshop out in Florida. I had never been into white women. I had mad love for my beautiful black queens, but she was feeling the kid. Maribel was one of those white girls who always wanted to please daddy, which didn't include being attracted to brothers.

Our last night out in Florida, after a night of drinking, she ended up back in my hotel room getting all nine inches of this dick. I woke up the next morning, and she was gone. When I went to the bathroom, that's when I noticed the condom was broken. I had no way to get in touch with her to let her know, and when I went to her hotel room, she had already checked out. Seven months later, I received a message request through Facebook from her, asking me to give her a call when I got a chance. I guess you already knew what the call was about. She informed me that she had just given birth to our daughter. She was born premature, weighing two pounds and nine ounces.

At the time, I wasn't ready for a baby. After a talk with my father, he convinced me to go out to Minnesota to see the baby, and he would accompany me. She was so little that I could've held her in one hand. She was hooked up to all these different tubes, and it was really hard for me to see. My father was there every step of the way. He had previous experience with Ruby being born premature and having to stay in the hospital for weeks. Ruby was way smaller than Mya by a pound. She was soon released from the hospital eight weeks later, and I made it my business to fly to Minnesota to be there when she came home.

Maribel's father wasn't a fan of me, and I really didn't give a shit. I wasn't trying to be with his daughter. I just wanted to be with my daughter. That's all that mattered to me. My mom threw me a baby shower, and it was a little weird because baby showers were usually for the mother. I ended up packing some of the stuff up that the family brought and bringing it to Minnesota. Maribel allowed her to come spend some time with me last summer. I was off on summer break, so I made sure I spent every minute with her. My mother and father spoiled the hell out of her the whole time. She was a beautiful mixed baby. She had naturally tanned skin and curly sandy brown hair. Her eyes were hazel like her mom's.

"She's actually coming for the summer again," I informed Jace.

"Cool... can't wait to see my little cutie," he responded.

"When you plan on making me a grandma?" Aunt Tiffany asked Jace.

"Never," Jace answered, making us laugh. Jace was the type to adore everyone else's kids, but he never wanted any of his own. My cousin was the definition of a man-whore. If you were to google man-whore, his picture would be the first thing that popped up.

"Hey, Jace."

"What up, Juanita?"

He nonchalantly greeted his ex-girlfriend who stood near his bike. He and Juanita were together for two years before he found out that she had partaken in a movie called *Dick Dynasty* where she was getting dubbed by four different niggas. After watching the video, Jace gave her the boot.

"Hi, Miss Tiffany."

Juanita greeted my aunt who gave her a fake smile. Then, she turned back to us.

"Oh, boy... let me get out of here. I'll see y'all at Pryce's going away party tomorrow."

My parents, Aunt Blaize, and Uncle Knight all decided it was time for them to take off as well.

"Uhh, y'all forgetting something," I said, stopping them in their tracks as they turned toward me.

"What are we forgetting?"

"Y'all kids... Ruby, Pryce, be gone."

"Boy, bye. I am grown. I'm eighteen," Ruby's smart ass responded.

"Well, I'll go. I got some more packing to do. Kumba tecchi wa," Pryce spoke in her and Bryce's twin language, followed by a kiss to his cheek. The two of them had always had this language they spoke since they were younger. I never knew what it was about until I got older and read about twins having their own language. The whole family could all be sitting together somewhere, and they would start talking in this language and start laughing. We all would look at each other,

9

trying to figure out what the joke was. Aunt Blaize was so used to it that she understood a little of what they were saying. When they started speaking, we all would turn to her to translate.

After all of the parents left, I stayed out there a little longer before making my way home to my girl, Genesis.

PRYCE'S GOING AWAY PARTY

PRYCE

I looked outside my bedroom window, and there were a lot of cars that flooded the driveway and spilled out into the street. Everyone had come to see me off on my journey as if I was leaving for a year. I was going on a three-week missionary trip to Africa … at least that was the story I told my parents. I was really going on an all-expense paid bae-cation with my boyfriend, whom they knew nothing about. Everyone looked at me as the innocent one because I was quiet, kept up my grades, and didn't really give them any problems. Between Kaylee, Bryce, and KJ, I was the perfect child, and I used that to my advantage. You know how they say that it's the quiet ones you have to watch out for? Well, that's true.

I was sixteen years old, about to be seventeen in a month, and dating a guy a few years older than me who I was in love with. I knew if my parents found out about me having a boyfriend, they would want to meet him. But, I knew if they did meet him, they would stop me from seeing him, and I would just die. I met him at church, and we'd been seeing each other since I was fifteen years old, but it didn't become sexual until I turned sixteen. I lost my virginity on the balcony of the church one night when I was supposed to be at a classmate's sleepover.

11

Because I was the good kid, my parents believed my every word. My dad was the easier of the two to convince, but my mother... she was suspicious of everything. I think it came from the abuse she suffered years back. She trusted no one that wasn't family. She was overly protective of her kids, so it took her some time before my dad and I were able to get her to agree to let me take the trip. My father was all for getting out and seeing the world, while my mother saw the dangers in everything.

My sister, Kaylee, moved to Paris a few years ago, and my mother cried for almost a year straight. She knew she didn't have too much say though, because Kaylee was twenty-six, and she was old enough to make her own decisions. I, on the other hand, still had to abide by the rules and continue to play innocent to gain my parents' trust.

Knock! Knock!

"Come in!" I shouted to whomever was knocking on my room door.

"Hey, baby. Your guests are arriving," my mom informed me as she poked her beautiful face in the room. My mom was probably one of the most beautiful women I knew. My family was full of beautiful women; my mom, my aunts, Tiffany and Camilla, my sister, Kaylee, and my cousin, Ruby... beautiful women surrounded by a bunch of overprotective men. I considered myself the ugly duckling compared to them.

"Okay, Mom, I'm coming down now."

"Okay."

She cried. I stood up off my bed and walked over to her.

"Ah, Mom, don't cry. I'll be fine. I'm going to make sure I FaceTime you every night."

"I know. I'm just scared. I'm a mom. I worry about all of my babies. I'll be fine though. You have everything packed?" she asked, stroking my hair and twirling my gray strand of hair around her finger like she did every chance she got.

"Yes, I have everything packed. You stop worrying so much. You're going to get worry lines. Just think of how great this will look on my college application."

"You're right. I need to look at the bigger picture. You're going to be okay."

"Exactly. Now let's go downstairs and party," I said, bumping my booty into hers. She wiped the tears from her face and then draped her arm over my shoulder as we walked out my bedroom and downstairs to join the party.

I wanted to get her out my room before she started checking my suitcase to make sure I packed everything and ended up coming across the brand-new lingerie I had just bought from Victoria's Secret.

I followed my mother down the stairs into the living room where my cousin, Nico, sat with his baby mama, Yvette, standing over him. I assumed by all the hand movements she was doing that they had to be arguing, or should I say, Yvette was arguing, and Nico was paying her zero mind. He just sat back, biting at his nails, looking up at her, and giving her the illusion that he was paying attention when he was most likely looking past her. Yvette's voice was so annoying. She reminded me of Teyanna Taylor's character in *Madea's Big Happy Family* with all the nagging she did. My cousin, Nico, wasn't the rowdy type at all, and that was because he stayed high as a kite. I think that was what was allowing him to remain calm right now.

"Hey, y'all."

I greeted the two of them, and they both turned.

"Hi," Yvette spoke with an attitude, causing me to jerk my neck.

"Lil' cuz," Nico said, jumping up quick and coming over to me. He draped his arm over my shoulders.

"Thank God y'all came down because I was about to clothesline that chick," he whispered, following us into the kitchen.

"Yeah right. You wouldn't bust a grape in a fruit fight."

"You right, but I will bust a bitch in her lip if she keeps talking reckless."

"So you just gon' leave her standing there?" I asked him.

"Yep. Yo, I'll be right back. Wait right here!" he yelled back at her as we walked into the kitchen toward the back door.

"You ain't going back. You are so wrong."

We both laughed. When we got outside in the backyard, the backyard was flooded with people; some family, some friends, and some people I barely knew who were only here because they knew my family threw some of the best parties. I spotted my best friends, Shirleen and Jo, sitting on the side of the pool, and of course they were in the boys' faces. I shook my head and walked over to them.

"Hey, ladies."

I greeted them once I reached the pool side.

"Hey, P," Shirleen greeted, standing up and giving me a hug. Jo stood up and hugged me as well, but she was eyeing something behind me. I turned around and automatically knew it was Nico. She'd always had a thing for my cousin. I told her to save herself the heartbreak because my cousin was not leaving his crazy ass baby mama. If a chick even looked at my cousin funny, Juanita jumped in boxing stance, but of course, she wasn't trying to hear what I was saying.

Jo was a little hoe on the low, which was funny because she was the preacher's kid. They say the preachers' kids are the ones that act out the most. In Jo's case, I would have to agree. She and I had been best friends since the third grade. We met Shirleen in the seventh grade when she moved from Cali and was transferred to our school. She was a little peculiar, but she grew out of it and started acting like a full bred ratchet ass Jersey chick.

"Okay, did you come here to see me or stare at my cousin?" I asked Jo.

"Oh, my bad, P," she said, giving me a hug.

"You know I came for you, but you also know I want your cousin… in my mouth," she whispered.

"You are so nasty. If you keep staring at him, you gon' catch a fist in your mouth. Juanita is in the living room."

"I don't give a shit about his baby mama. I'm trifling like that. Just look at him. He walks like he's hung like a walrus."

"Oh my God. I can't listen to this. I'll be back," I said, walking away from them and over by my dad, Uncle Troy, and Uncle Swift.

"What's up, OMG's?" I greeted as I sat down on my daddy's lap.

"Girl, ain't nothing about us old," Uncle Troy said. They didn't like when I called them the OMG's which stood for Old Man Gang. They all were in their mid to late forties. Besides the little bit of gray hair that seasoned Uncle Troy who was the oldest, they all could be mistaken as being in their early thirties.

"Real talk. We still can get it in," my dad responded.

"I definitely don't want to know what you mean by that."

"No you don't, baby girl. That's between me and your mama. You all packed?"

"Yes, I'm packed. Mom made sure of that."

"You packed some food? I don't want my baby out there starving."

"Daddy, you sound like your wife now. I'm not going to starve. I will be just fine."

"I got one of my baby girls out in Paris, and the other one about to go to Africa. Now if only I could get rid of them two nugget head brothers of yours, me and wifey can walk around naked again."

"Eww... TMI, dude," I said, covering my ears. My father believed that as a family, we should be open and tell each other everything. He was the only one who exercised that rule. He was a little too open about the wrong things.

"Yo, yo, yo, what's up, y'all? Hey, Pops," Ruby greeted us, coming over and sitting on her father's lap. Although we wanted to be treated like adults, Ruby and I were daddy's girls. Even as we sat here on our fathers' laps in front of a backyard full of people, we felt no shame in our game.

"Where you coming from, little girl, and why the hell it smells like your clothes were washed in THC laundry detergent?" Uncle Troy asked Ruby, who played dumb and sniffed at her clothes.

"I don't know. Ask ya wife. She washes my clothes," Ruby responded, picking up Uncle Troy's Corona bottle and attempting to sip from it, but she

was deterred by Uncle Troy grabbing the bottle. I laughed. Ruby was a handful. Everyone told her she acted like her GG.

Her great grandmother, who we all called G-ma, was a mess. She was one of the funniest people I knew. Growing up, she considered my siblings and myself as her great grands as well. She didn't treat us

15

no different than she did her real great grands. Although it wasn't apparent, we all knew Ruby was her favorite, and that's because she was her mini-me.

"Don't play with me, Diavion."

"Alright, I was chilling with Trey, and the smell must've gotten in my clothes," she admitted. Trey was our cousin. Uncle Troy and Aunt Camilla raised him after his father was killed. Trey was like the black sheep of the family. He fell in with the wrong crowd a few years ago. Uncle Troy and Aunt Camilla found out he was selling drugs, and they gave him an ultimatum. Either he stopped selling, or he had to leave their home. He decided to leave. He came around every now and then, caused a commotion, and then he would leave. I think he got a rise out of the drama he caused.

"What I tell you about hanging around Trey?" Uncle Troy asked, taking a sip from his beer. You could tell he was now bothered.

"He's my cousin. You can't raise us up together and then tell me to just forget about him. He was practically my damn brother."

"You watch ya damn mouth, little girl, and if I say I don't want you hanging around him, then that's what you better do. You don't know what the fuck that boy out in them streets doing, and you don't need to be getting mixed up with none of that shit," Uncle Troy stated. Ruby sucked her teeth.

"I'm out of here," Ruby said, jumping off her father's lap.

"Yo' ass better not leave this damn backyard."

Ruby ignored him and walked over by Malachi. Whenever she got mad at her father, she went and crawled up under her big brother who also babied her.

"I'm about to ship her little ass off to Africa, right along with you, niece."

"Uhh, no. I don't think the motherland can handle her," I joked.

KAYLEE

I pulled up in front of my family's home. Jean Claude and I had just gotten off the plane about an hour ago. Our visit was a surprise. No one knew we were flying in. I wanted to bid my little sister farewell and safe travels, and a little part of me missed my family dearly.

Jean Claude and I were engaged and currently planning our wedding for next year. To say I was happy would be an overstatement. In the beginning of our relationship, things were great. I met Jean Claude a few months after I moved to Paris. I was assisting on a fashion show, and Jean Claude was the photographer covering the show. He approached me and asked me on a date. I was new here and looking forward to making friends.

Things were pretty good for the first year of dating. Then, we got engaged, and that's when the true Jean Claude revealed his ugly head. He showed me a side I had never seen before, but by then, I was in too deep. I was so in love with him that when he hit me the first time, I blamed myself and continued to blame myself every time after that. I really believed that it was something that I was doing that was causing him to react this way. I tried changing my ways, changing the way I dressed, and making sure he was fed, but that didn't change him. He was a monster.

I pulled the overhead mirror down and started touching up my makeup. I felt Jean Claude's eyes on me. I looked over at him.

"What's wrong?" I asked him.

"What you getting all cute for? Who you trying to impress in there?" he questioned.

"What? No one. I'm trying to cover up these bruises on my neck that you made. If my family was to see these, trust me, you won't be walking out that backyard."

He rolled his eyes and went back to looking out the window until I was done applying my makeup.

"Okay, let's go," I said, stepping out of the car. I had on my strapless floral dress that fit my form perfectly. I mean, it should. I designed it just for me. It had a split that came up mid-thigh, the back was strappy and showed my back just a little, and some summer time wedges. My hair was in a high ponytail on the top of my head. Although it was about eighty degrees out today, I still wrapped a scarf around my neck to hide Jean Claude's handprint from when he choked me up in the airplane's bathroom. He got upset because I insulted the ascot that he was wearing. I was just speaking the truth. He looked like a damn fool.

We walked into the house, and it was empty, so we immediately went out to the backyard. I slid the door open, and the backyard was packed, but my family was all sitting at the tables near the door.

"Bonjour, la famille," I shouted in French, getting their attention.

"Ahhh, Kaylee!" Pryce yelled, jumping off my father's lap and running toward me. I couldn't believe how much she'd grown from being that annoying little sister who wanted to wear my clothes, to the beautiful young lady before me. When she got to me, she hugged me tightly as we both stood there embracing each other.

"Oh my God, Kaylee. Why didn't you tell me you were flying in?" my crying mother said, walking up to me and giving me a tight hug. My mother was such a cry baby, but she was tough as nails.

"Please say you're home for good," she begged.

"No, Mom. I just wanted to come say bye to Pryce," I answered. She started crying harder.

"Would it make you feel better if we stayed for a few days?"

"Yes."

She wiped her face.

"I'm sorry. Hi Jean."

She greeted him with a hug.

"You're still as handsome as ever."

"Thank you, Mrs. Knight. You're still as lovely as ever, even with a face full of tears," he responded in his French accent.

I spotted my dad walking toward me, so like the daddy's girl I was, I ran to him and jumped in his arms. I missed him the most. My dad always made me feel safe when I was around him. I felt like I could tell him anything, but I knew I couldn't tell him about the abuse I was experiencing in my relationship. Although Jean Claude looked innocent, he was a very dangerous man with many connections, so getting away from him wouldn't be easy.

"I missed you so much, baby girl."

"I missed you too, Daddy."

He finally released me from his hug and looked me over. I was happy I had this scarf around my neck because he would have definitely seen the bruise around my neck and this party would have gotten shut down quickly. Jean Claude would have had my dad, uncles, brother and cousins on his ass in two seconds. Let's not forget my mother and Aunt Camilla. Those two were two strong women. They could move a mountain alone if need be.

I made my rotations around the backyard, saying "hi" to all of my family members. I looked over to where Jean Claude was sitting, looking as if he would have preferred to be somewhere else. I rolled my eyes and continued with my business. I wasn't about to let him ruin my time with my family.

Whenever we were around his family, he always expected me to be happy and involved and interact with his family, who I knew didn't like me much. I figured it was because of my skin tone. He was blind to the fact, but I wasn't. They wanted their son with someone who was the same complexion as them.

I walked over to where my cousin, Malachi, and his friends were sitting.

"Cuzzo," I greeted, hugging him from behind and kissing him on the cheek.

"Aye, get over here, beautiful girl," he said, standing up and pulling me in for a hug. Wild child Ruby jumped out the pool and was coming close to me with her arms open. She was dripping wet, so I held out my hand out to keep some distance between us so that she wouldn't get me wet.

"Come on, bougie butt. Give your favorite little cousin a hug," she said with a smile.

"Hell no, Ruby. Get a towel first."

"Nope," she said, running up on me and giving me a hug, getting my dress wet. When she was done, she ran back and jumped in the pool. Malachi had pulled my chair next to his, and I sat down. I noticed a familiar back facing me. I couldn't forget that back even if I tried. I spent many nights admiring that beautifully sculpted back.

"Hello, Enzo," I greeted. He turned around slightly and gave me a head nod.

"What's up, Kaylee," he said, turning back around to the pool like he couldn't care less for my presence, but I knew that was all an act. He and I had a thing before I left for France. No one really knew about us but Malachi. Enzo and Malachi had been best friends since forever. Although I was two years older than them, I watched as they grew up. Once Enzo turned eighteen, I started watching him in a different way. That kid grew into one fine ass man. He had a chocolate skin tone, pearly white teeth, thick black wavy hair, and not to mention he'd had a six pack since he was like ten. We became intimate on his twentieth birthday. Malachi had thrown him a birthday party one summer, and I had a little bit too much to drink, but I wasn't incoherent. I mistakenly walked into the bathroom without knocking on the door, and Enzo was in there using the bathroom. Instead of walking back out of the bathroom, I just stood there wide eyed and continued to watch his thick chocolate penis do what it do. When I looked up, he was looking at me smiling and biting on his bottom lip.

"Can I help you with something, Kaylee?" he asked, causing me to break my daze. He shook off his penis and stuffed it back in his shorts, but never zipped or buttoned them back up.

"Maybe you can," I stated. He washed his hands and started walking toward me. I started backing up until I couldn't go anymore and bumped into the door. His six-foot frame stood over me, and the liquor took control. I dug my hands down his open shorts and grabbed a handful of his penis, and it was all over from there. He picked me up, ripped the crotch part of my panties, and fucked me right there against the door.

Our sexual relationship went on for years, to a point where I ended up pregnant. Against Enzo's wishes, I went and got an abortion which ended our secret rendezvous. He wanted me to keep it, but I had plans that didn't involve a baby on my hip... not to mention the disappointment from my parents. As good as the sex was, I wasn't ready to be anybody's baby mama. Just thinking about the sex Enzo and I shared had me hot. I had to go cool off.

"I'll be back. I have to go to the bathroom. It was a long flight," I said, excusing myself as I rushed into the house and downstairs to the bathroom. I grabbed a washcloth and ran it under cold water. Then, I placed it on my head and waited. A minute later, there was a knock on the door. I smiled, set the washcloth down, and went and opened the door. I was hoping he'd caught the hint.

"Hey," I greeted him. He said nothing. He just walked into the bathroom, shutting the door and locking it. I hiked my skirt up just a little because I knew how he turned into a savage, and I'd paid almost three hundred dollars for this dress. I didn't want him to rip it.

He lifted me on to the sink as he stared deep into my eyes. He cupped my face in his hands as he placed his lips on top of my mine. I parted my lips, allowing his tongue access into my mouth. His hands roamed my thighs as he pushed my dress up higher. He pulled my panties to the side as his fingers roamed up and down the slit of my cooch before his finger slid inside me.

"You missed me?" he finally spoke.

"Oui," I answered in French, meaning yes.

"You missed me?" I asked, already knowing the answer.

"Nope. I can't miss someone who bounced on me three years ago and came back engaged."

"Do you still love me?"

"I'll always love you, Kaylee," he answered. I grabbed his face and kissed him passionately. I slid my panties down and kicked them off. I loosened up his trunks and pulled out his huge penis that I missed. I pulled him closer to me as I inserted his head inside my opening.

"Shit, Kaylee," he moaned into my neck as he pushed in and out of me. He picked me up off the sink as he sat down on the toilet with me on top of him. I rode him right there on the toilet while my parents and fiancé sat right outside.

～

TWENTY MINUTES LATER, I had freshened myself up and was walking out the bathroom to go back out to the backyard. I wasn't paying attention to where I was walking. I was too busy ironing the wrinkles out my dress with hands, and I ran into someone. I looked up, and it was Jean Claude.

"Hey, are you heading to the bathroom?" I asked him nervously.

"Yes, and looking for you. Where have you been all this time?"

"I wasn't gone for too long. I just had to use the bathroom," I lied.

"Really?" he questioned. His eyes were dead, which was kind of scary. Normally, when he had this look in his eyes, it meant an ass whopping was to follow. I knew he wasn't stupid enough to hit me with my whole family only feet away.

He leaned in close to me, and I jumped slightly. He grabbed my scarf, pulled me closer, and started sniffing me. I became nervous. I knew I had Enzo's scent on me.

He stood back up and, once again, gave me the look. Then, he walked around me and into the bathroom. I ran back up the stairs into the backyard. I decided to go sit by my mother and aunts. I already knew what the conversation was going to be about.

"What y'all old ladies over here talking about?" I asked, sitting down in one of the unoccupied seats.

"Voulez vous coucher avec moi," Aunt Camilla answered, unknown to what she had just asked me.

"If you weren't my aunt, maybe I would consider it," I answered.

"What the hell did I just say?" she asked, making me laugh.

"You asked if I wanted to sleep with you."

"Oh, damn. How do you say eat in French?" Camilla asked.

"Mon-zhee, but you spell it like you would spell manager. Why?"

"Thinking about teaching Beauty and the Beast French," Aunt Camilla said talking about her two dogs she had at home. "Anyway, when is the wedding?".

"What wedding?" I asked then caught myself.

"I mean, it's next year."

The three of them gave me a funny look.

"Is everything okay with you and Jean Claude?" my mom asked. I wanted to tell her no and how bad I wanted to come back home, but I knew she would start asking questions that, if I answered, would get me hurt as well as them.

"Yes, Mom, everything is okay."

I took a water bottle out of the bucket of ice.

"Then what was that little slip up just now? No happy bride forgets about their wedding. Something's not right, but you'll tell me when you're ready."

"Seriously, everything is good. I just got distracted," I explained, taking a sip of water.

"By what, a half-naked Enzo?" Ruby asked, coming out of nowhere and sitting at the table with us. I damn near choked on the water that I had just sipped.

"What? No, Ruby. Why would you say that?" I asked her, confused as to how she knew about Enzo and me.

"I'm very, very observant. You think I didn't notice the two of you leave at the same time not too long ago. Uh huh, it's all good. Your secret is safe with me."

Everyone was now looking at me. I was visibly embarrassed. I looked at Ruby through squinted eyes.

"You know nothing, you little Chucky doll," I said and started to walk away.

"Aye, Kaylee!" she called.

"What?"

I turned around with an attitude.

"How your dress get ripped? Enzo got a little rough?"

"None of your business," I answered and stormed away.

LIL' RUBY

$\mathcal{I}$ sat there laughing at the way Kaylee stormed away. Her ass knew she was caught. She and Enzo weren't a secret to anyone but her Frenchy fiancé that sat in the corner acting like he was better than everyone. I started to go over there and fuck with him, but my mother told me not to. If there was one person I was scared of, it was my crazy ass mother. I'd heard stories about my mother from back in the early days. My devilish ways had nothing on the shit I heard about her. Hyenas, machetes, spider venoms… my mother was lethal, but looking at her, you would have never guessed.

I got smart with my mother once, and she threatened to feed me to her Bullmastiff/Pitbull mix she called Beauty and the Beast. Those dogs were creepy as fuck. I don't think I'd ever seen them eat, but they were big as a damn house, and they only listened to my mother. They practically had their own house. Their kennel was kept outside, and it was bigger than most people's apartments. Every now and then, I would go and fuck with them, but they just sat there staring at me like I was food.

Speaking of staring at someone like they were food, I looked over at the table where my dad and uncles were sitting, and that bitch, Genesis, was sitting over there staring at my dad like he was a well fried pork chop. This wasn't the first time I caught the bitch flirting with death.

Genesis was Malachi's girlfriend. She was the Great Value version of Kelly Rowland if you asked me. She and my brother had been together for almost a year. I often caught her giving my dad the hungry eyes, but he paid no attention to her. I still felt like she was disrespecting my mother, and I didn't play that shit.

I stood up from the table, walked over to my father, and sat on his lap, facing Genesis.

"What up, fish. I mean, sis?" I greeted, smiling in her face. I felt my dad lightly tap me on the back. He knew I didn't like when she was up in his face. If you asked me, this bitch was only with my brother to get a chance to see my father every day.

"Hello, Diavion," she responded with a little attitude.

"It's Ruby to you. Why you the only chick over here with all these married men?"

"I'm chilling. Why? It's something wrong with me being over here?" she asked.

"No, but it's something wrong with you being all up in my dad's face. Ain't ya man over there? How about you go be up in his face."

"Diavion, cut it out," my father scolded. I turned around and looked at him like I was the parent scolding him.

"It's all good. Maybe I will go see what my man is up to," she said, getting up and adding an extra twist in her hips as she walked away.

"Ruby, you's a menace."

Uncle Knight laughed.

"Just ridding the world of hoes, one skank at a time. As you were, gentleman."

I jumped up from my dad's lap and went on about my business. After I was done terrorizing my family, I said goodbye to Pryce once again before I decided to split. I got in my 2016 Honda Accord and started it up. I decided to go over to my boyfriend, Jayon's, crib and pay him a visit. I knew my parents weren't going to be at the party for much longer, and once they got home, they were going to be expecting me home as well. Jayon lived in the Fourth Ward section of

Paterson, directly in the middle of the hood. If my parents knew where I was hanging, the both of them would kick down every door on the Fourth looking for me. They knew how cray it got in the area, but personally, I wasn't scared.

I pulled out my phone and called Jayon, but it went straight to voicemail like he had his phone cut off, so I decided to just show up. I had a key, so I figured it was okay for me to do so. Jayon was twenty-one years old. He was a small-time drug dealer that hung with my cousin, Trey. That was how Jayon and I met. We'd been kicking it for about a year now, and within that year, I'd had to lay a few bitches out behind him. I don't think there was a bitch stupid enough to still try and talk to him.

About five minutes later, I was pulling up in front of his apartment building. His car was out here, so I knew he had to be close by. He was probably on the block somewhere. I made sure to grab my key before getting out of the car. My parents knew nothing about Jayon. They may have thought I was gay because I was a little rough around the edges, and I was okay with them thinking that. They weren't too far off. I had a girl go down on me once. It was unexpected though. I think my parents would've been happy if I was, in fact, gay.

I entered the apartment and put my bag and keys down. The house was dark, but there was a light escaping from under the bedroom door. I heard A Boogie coming from the bedroom. I walked closer to the door and pushed it open slightly. The first thing I noticed was a woman's clothing on the floor. I looked up in the bed, and there was a chick on top of Jayon, riding him like he was a bucking bull. What I couldn't take my eyes off were her flappy ass titties as they bounced up and down and damn near smacked her in the face.

Normally, I would have jumped on that bed and started stomping both of them out, but I had something better. I was sick of this shit. I was about to teach him a lesson once and for all.

I slowly backed out of the room and quietly closed the door behind me. When I got back out into the living room, I grabbed my bag and my keys and left the apartment. I got back in my car and drove around the corner to the gas station. I got the gas container from inside my trunk and paid for a half of gallon of gas. Then, I quickly ran into the Family Dollar that was right around the corner and grabbed a mason jar, a lighter, and some Gorilla Glue.

When I got back to the apartment, I sat in my car, preparing my bomb. I warned this nigga not to fuck with me, and he failed to take my warning. I grabbed the Gorilla Glue and my homemade bomb, and stepped out the car. When I got up the stairs, I unlocked the apartment door, and just like before, it was still dark. I walked into the apartment, crept to the bedroom, and looked in. They were both asleep.

Why were niggas so stupid? Why would you give a chick the key to your apartment just to bring another bitch in there and fall asleep with the hoe? *Wrong move, buddy.*

I turned back to the door and proceeded to place Gorilla Glue on the door. I lit the cloth that hung out the jar with the gasoline, threw it into the apartment, and closed the door. I held it shut as hard as I could, giving the glue time to set before I ran back out of the building and jumped in my car. I looked up at the living room window and could see the flames illuminating the living room. I smiled.

Before I left, I made sure to leave him a little note on the windshield of his car.

～

I GOT home around 11 o'clock. The house appeared to be quiet, but that was just the fact that this house was huge, and everyone sort of had their own wing of the house. Malachi and Trey used to share the guest house, but since Trey decided to leave, Malachi decided to turn the guest house into his own little bachelor pad. You couldn't really call it a bachelor's pad, because his girlfriend, Genesis, practically lived there too.

Mega and I shared one end, and my mother and father were all the way on the other end of the house. Mega was always at the gym training, so that left me alone most of the time, which I didn't mind. At least I didn't have to worry about him complaining about my trap music.

I dropped my bag in the middle of the floor and went into the kitchen. I was looking through the refrigerator when I heard my mom and dad laughing as they walked into the kitchen.

"When did you get home?" my father asked as they both waked into the kitchen.

"Like five minutes ago," I answered, taking a Corona from the refrigerator and popping it open. My father walked around the island and snatched the bottle from my lips just as I was about to take a sip. I sucked my teeth.

"Where you coming from?" he asked.

"From burning someone's house down," I answered, jumping on the countertop and grabbing an apple out the fruit bowl.

"Funny."

I shrugged my shoulders. He didn't have to believe me. They never did, which was fine with me. At least if I got caught, they couldn't say I didn't tell them. Mega and Malachi had finally walked into the house as we were all in the kitchen.

"Ding dong, the loser's home."

I mocked my little brother, Mega. He was the better child out of the three. I couldn't say he was spoiled, because we were all spoiled by our parents. We typically got whatever we wanted if we could provide a reasonable explanation for wanting it. I wanted a gun once, and when they asked me why I wanted a gun, I explained that I needed to run up on a few bitches on the block. My mother taught me how to shoot a gun when I was thirteen, so I don't know why they wouldn't trust me with a gun.

"Shut up, dike," he responded, making everyone but me laugh as he dug into his nasty ass gym bag.

"Ya mother," I said, throwing my half-bitten apple at him that he managed to duck before it collided with his head.

"Watch ya mouth, little girl, before I smack it off your face," my mother threatened.

"Chill, Ma—" I started to say before something hit me in the face. I stopped talking and looked down on the floor at what had just hit me. It was Mega's jock strap. I was heated, not because he threw something at me, but because it was something that was on his dick, and it had just touched my lip.

"You gay motherfucker," I said, jumping down off the countertop and running toward him, jumping on his back. I started punching him in his head.

"Ruby, what I tell you about punching my baby in his head!" my mother yelled, but I wasn't paying her no mind. I wrapped my arms around his neck and locked him in a headlock until he brought his arm up and punched me in the forehead, causing me to loosen my grip around his neck.

"So y'all not gon' break them up?" I heard Malachi ask my parents who both just sat there paying us no mind. They were used to Mega and I fighting, which didn't end until someone broke us up, or we just got tired and just called it a truce.

"Nope, they'll get tired," my father responded, never looking up from his phone. Mega spun me around, and I was now hanging onto him like a spider monkey. I was hitting him wherever I could find an opening on his body. My little brother was stocky and strong as shit. I think he bench pressed more than my body weight.

At fifteen years old, he was one of the best running backs in the state of New Jersey. He was only in the tenth grade and had scouts already eyeing him. Although Mega and I fought all the time, I was one of his biggest fans. I think it was me beating him up all the time that made him tough.

"They gon' be here forever."

Malachi came over and tried to pull me off, but I wasn't letting go... that was until he started tickling me under my arms, and I just surrendered. I hated being tickled. Malachi walked me over to my father and threw me in his lap. My father wrapped his arm around my neck, and this time, he had me in a headlock.

"What I tell you about cursing in this house?" he asked, pressing his knuckles in my forehead.

"Ouuch, I didn't curse," I said, loosening his grip around my neck and standing up off his lap. I walked over to the fridge and got a water.

"What took y'all so long to get back from the school?" my mother asked.

"It didn't take us that long. There was a little detour because of some fire on the 4th," Malachi answered. I choked on my water, getting everyone's attention. They all looked at me.

"On that note, I'm going to bed," I said, about to walk out the kitchen.

"Hold the hell up. Get yo' little ass back in here," my father voiced. *Shit!* I cursed in my head. I knew this wasn't gon' be good.

MALACHI

フ

*A*fter I was done talking with my parents and crazy ass
siblings, I decided to take it down for the night. I walked
through the backyard to get to the guest house. I noticed the lights
still on, which meant Genesis was still up. Good. That meant I could
take a dive in those guts before I knocked out.

I walked in the house and was welcomed by her perfume. It only
intensified my erection even more. I loved a woman that kept herself
looking and smelling nice. I couldn't stand a funky bitch. Genesis was
beautiful to me, although Ruby thought otherwise. She called her a
Kelly Rowland knockoff. Ruby wasn't really a fan of Genesis. She felt
like she was always flirting with our father. If she was, I would find
out sooner or later, but in the meantime, I was gon' wear that pussy
out until I found her replacement.

"Jenny from the block... where you at, girl?" I called. I kicked off
my shoes as I made my way through the house. I walked into the
bedroom, and she was lying in the bed, looking through her phone. I
started stripping down until I stood in nothing but my boxers.

I climbed on the bed and crawled between her thighs. She had
nothing on but my Giants jersey. I shifted down and lifted the jersey
up, putting my head under it. I kissed her flat stomach and made my

32

way up to her titties, cupping one in my hand and sucking her nipple. One of Genesis's areoles was shaped like a heart. I thought it was cute. I grabbed the other titty and did the same thing before I started kissing up her long neck. Her neck was the spot that, once stimulated, drove her crazy.

She removed the jersey, pulling it over her head. I kissed down to her belly button, and I felt her pushing at my head. I knew what that meant. She wanted me to get cookie monster on that pussy, and that's exactly what happened. One of the many things I prided myself on was my pussy eating skills. I could make a bitch tap out in seconds. Only the grown and sexy could handle this tongue ride. Sadly, Genesis wasn't one.

I was only down here for about thirty seconds before her body started shaking, and she was pushing my head away. I got up on my knees and pulled down my boxer briefs. My dick was brick hard, and I was ready to get it wet. I reached over to the side dresser, pulled out a condom, and carefully rolled it down my dick. I wanted to avoid any nips and rips. I liked Genesis, but I wasn't trying to have a kid with her.

Once I had the condom on, I entered her slowly and started grinding on her G-spot, getting the kitty extra wet. I grabbed onto her small waist, and I pumped in and out of her. Watching her titties bounce as I started slamming into her pussy had me on one hundred. I started beating the pussy all the way up. That's one thing I liked about Genesis. She could handle every blow I threw in her pussy, and she brought it back harder. She took dick like a porn star.

I turned her around and started hitting it from the back. She grabbed on to her ass cheeks and spread them wide so that I was able to see her hairless asshole. I licked my thumb and did what any man would. I placed my thumb right in her ass, and she loved every minute of it.

We were getting it in so heavy that I didn't even realize the bed was moving. It started out against the wall and was now in the middle of the bedroom. I didn't care. I just kept on fucking and focusing on busting that first nut.

Genesis reached under her body and started massaging my balls. That's all it took for me to bust a nut so hard that the shit should have broken through the condom. I let her go, and we both fell on to the bed exhausted, breathing rapidly, and trying to catch our breath.

With my eyes closed, I searched the bed for my phone. I felt a phone and picked it up. It wasn't mine. It was Genesis's. When I picked the phone up, the first thing that popped up was a zoomed in picture of my father.

"Why do you have a picture of my pops?" I asked, turning the phone toward her.

"It was a mistake picture. I was deleting pictures out my phone before you came in," she answered.

"Oh," I said, deleting the picture for her and then handing her back her phone. I laid there until it was time for round two.

~

I WOKE up early the next morning, washed, and got dressed. It was a Sunday morning, and instead of getting some rest before I had to go deal with these hardheaded ass kids, I told Enzo I would help him at the daycare. Enzo worked as an independent contractor for privately owned businesses. He could build a house from the ground up. My mother had him doing some renovations at one of the daycares. Since she had opened her first daycare, she had successfully opened up three more since. Enzo was building an office in one of the locations for the director there, and he needed help installing the windows.

When I left out of the house, Genesis was still sleeping. She would be getting up soon. She usually went to church on Sundays, but after that beating I put on that ass last night, I doubted if she would get up in time. There had been many times she had tried to get me to go to church with her, but I wasn't the church going type. I liked to use my Sundays as a day of healing from the hangover from Saturday nights.

I ran into my mother as I was exiting the house. She was walking toward the kennels to see Beauty and Beast.

"Yo, crazy lady," I called, getting her attention.

"Hey, baby."

She greeted me with a smile, turned directions, and started walking toward me. She was probably coming from the gym, seeing as though she had on her workout gear. I took in my mom's appearance. My mom had the looks and shape of a woman in her late twenties. She was the epitome of a black goddess if you asked me. She had on her Nike yoga pants with the matching sports bra that showed off her flat and toned stomach. You would have never guessed she had any kids.

Years ago, my dad was able to stop her from wearing weave and to embrace her natural hair. Her hair was braided in one braid down the middle that touched the middle of her back, just above her back dimples. It was a little disturbing to me because I found them sexy on women for some reason. My mom's hips, butt, and thigh ratio was on point. There wasn't a day that went by that niggas my age didn't try to holla at my mom. My dad was a lucky man. I hoped to one day find a woman as bad and loyal to make mine forever. Genesis wasn't it. I knew that for a fact.

"Where you headed?" she asked while giving me a hug.

"To give Enzo a hand at the daycare. Thanks for giving him the job. He really needed it," I said. Enzo was an independent contractor, but business hadn't really been booming for him lately. I had him talk with my mother about putting in some work around the daycares. He was skilled, and my parents were mysteriously loaded. I never asked questions about their finances, because it was none of my business.

"You don't have to thank me. Enzo is like a son to me. He should have told me he was struggling when I opened the last two locations. Those places needed major work, and I would have rather given him the money than a stranger."

"He's a man, Ma. He's not going to admit he needs help."

"Yeah... well, you men need to know when to put those egos to the side and start opening those mouths."

"You right. Where were you going... to play with your devil dogs?" I joked.

"Don't talk about my babies like that. They are only evil when I need them to be. You should come spend some time with them. I'm going to set a date for the four of us," she mentioned.

"I'll pass. I swear I think you feed them people."

She flashed a wicked smile and put her finger up to her mouth, signaling to keep quiet.

"You are a weird woman, but I love you to death," I said, kissing her on the cheek and walking away.

"I love you more. I'll have my people get in touch with ya people so that we can schedule that date, alright?" she voiced from behind me.

"Bye, Ma," I said as I continued to walk toward the house. I entered through the back door and into the kitchen. My dad and Ruby were there. As always, Ruby had her ass planted on top of the counter. She didn't sit at the kitchen table like regular people. The countertop was her kitchen table.

"What up, bum?" I said, smacking her in the knee as I walked by, causing her fall off the countertop.

"Come on, step child," she called. We all knew that Camilla wasn't my birth mother, but that didn't make her less of a mother to me. For that reason Ruby called me Step child or Half breed.

Ruby was forever fucking with somebody, trying to get under their skin. She was very antagonistic like that, but I ignored the little demon seed. My sister was like a Naked Lady plant, pretty but poisonous… the miniature version of my mother but worse. Ruby caused havoc everywhere she went. It was a good thing she knew how to defend herself because she was forever talking shit. I'm sure people stayed wanting to knock her in the mouth.

"What up, T-money?" I greeted my Pops, sitting down at the table next to him. I grabbed a plate and loaded it with a few pieces of bacon and some homemade fries.

"Shit, going over some of the numbers from the clubs. I gotta find a way to generate more money at the Miami location."

"Turn it into a strip club. Naked bitches bring in the most money."

He looked up at me and then over to Ruby who was all in my mouth.

"Watch ya mouth around your sister," he warned, going back to looking over his books.

"I'm telling you the truth though. It's in the perfect location to flip it into a strip joint for men and women."

"It sounds like a good idea. I'll look into it. Where you going this early in the morning?" he asked.

"Meet up with Enzo at the daycare. Mom has him doing some renovations."

"Cool."

"Did he tell you about him and Kaylee yesterday?" Ruby questioned.

"Don't you ever mind yo' business, little girl?" I asked her.

"Nope, I try hard not to," she answered as I shook my head.

Kaylee and Enzo had been fucking around for some time now. It was supposed to be something on the low, but I knew about it from Enzo telling me. Ruby's little ass just watched and observed everything. I actually liked the thought of Enzo being with my cousin. They were perfect for each other, but Kaylee had other plans in Paris. I got bad vibes from that Frenchy dude. It was something about the way he just sat there not trying to socialize or get in with the family. Aunt Blaize liked him for some reason.

I continued to eat my food. When I was done, I left out and drove to the daycare.

～

"BOB THE BUILDER," I said upon entering the door of the daycare.

"What up, nigga?" he greeted, giving me pound.

"Shit, what you in here doing?"

"Trying to even out this window. Yo, do that look even?" he asked me, pointing to the window.

"Yeah, it's good. What you need my help with?" I asked him. There was a knock on the door, and we both turned and looked. There stood a sight for sore eyes. She had to stand about five feet seven inches tall, and had 150 pounds packed in all the right places. Her skin was the color of cocoa, her lips were thick. She looked like the chick that played Tony Childs on the TV show *Girlfriends*. I looked over at Enzo who gave me the go ahead. That was something we did since we were younger. If we were both feeling the girl, then neither one of us would holla. Kaylee was back, so I knew he wasn't looking at home girl like that. His mind was probably plotting on how to get Kaylee to stay here in Jersey and not go back to Paris. He was in love with my cousin, but I wasn't sure if she felt the same way for him.

"Hello," she greeted.

"Hello, beautiful. Can I help you with something?" I asked her.

"Oh, I'm Rhyes. Ms. Camilla told me to stop by and give you guys some paint suggestions for my office."

"Your office?" I questioned.

"Yes, this will be my office once you guys are done."

"You're the director?"

"Yes, I am."

"I'm Malachi, Camil—"

"You're Ms. Camilla's son. She speaks of you all the time, and she has pictures all over her office."

"Oh, really? That's not fair. Now I feel like you know me more than I know you. We have to even the score."

She laughed.

"Trust me. I don't know much."

"Do you want to get to know more?" I flirted.

"Umm, I would like to, but I don't think mixing business with pleasure is a good idea."

"You ain't in business with me. You in business with my moms."

"Exactly... your mom is crazy about her kids, and I love my job."

"My mom is harmless. She may be crazy about her kids, but if we're happy, then she's happy. A date with you would make me incredibly happy."

She stood there smiling and then turned to walk away, leaving me standing there.

"I guess you need to get ya game up, big homie," Enzo joked. I gave him the finger.

"Maybe you need to get ya game up and stop waiting on my cousin, nigga."

"Here," I heard Rhyes voice behind me. I turned around, and she was handing me a piece of paper. I looked down at it, and it had her name and number on it. The way her name was spelled was cute and different. It was pronounced Reese but spelled Rhyes.

"Hit me up, and we can discuss going on a date."

"I'll do that," I said, putting the paper in my pocket.

"Have a good day, Malachi."

"You do the same, Rhyes."

She walked out the office, and I stood there staring at the empty door for a minute, wishing she was still standing there.

"Damn, she's bad," I said out loud.

"She's cute, but what about the one you got at home?"

"What about her? She's only a filler for now until I find the one," I answered.

"The one, huh? Speaking of the one, Kaylee ever said anything to you about ol' boy putting his hands on her. Yesterday, I noticed marks on her neck. It looked like she tried to cover it with that scarf she was wearing," Enzo mentioned.

"Nah, she never said anything. I doubt if she would say something if he was putting his hands on her. What you was doing that close to her neck anyway, nigga?"

He chuckled.

"Mind ya damn business, and get to work."

"It ain't me. It's my nosey ass little sister. You know she got eyes every damn where, so if y'all trying to keep this thing under wraps, then keep away from where Ruby's ass is. You know how she likes to run her mouth."

He shook his head and went back to doing what he was doing. I was going to make a mental note to sit down and have a conversation with Kaylee before she went back to Paris with dude.

PRYCE

$\mathcal{W}$e pulled up to the airport, and my mother immediately started crying. I rolled my eyes because this was getting out of hand. I wondered how she was going to act when I moved out. I don't need to wonder. I had seen the way she reacted when Kaylee was leaving for the first time. I hopped out of the car, walking around to the trunk. My father came around there as well to help me with my luggage.

"Don't worry about your mother. She'll be aight. You go out there and enjoy yourself, alright?"

"I will, dad. I'll be fine."

"Where is the church group meeting you at?" he asked.

"By the boarding terminal. I can find my way," I said, trying to get him to leave.

"Nope, I'm staying until you get on that plane."

I smiled but rolled my eyes as I turned around. I really didn't need them walking me to my gate.

After I checked my bags, I sat at Starbucks with my parents. I didn't want them sitting at the gate and have them asking questions when they didn't see anyone else from the church. About twenty minutes later, I heard them call my gate. I grabbed my carry on and rushed to the gate.

"Where is everyone else?" my dad asked just as I expected.

"They're all probably on the plane already. It seems like I'm the last one."

"Oh no you're not. There's Pastor Jonas," my mother said, causing my heart to jump. I turned and looked to where she was pointing. He was walking over to us in his down clothes. I was used to seeing him in his suit, but today he looked un-Pastor like.

"Hello, Pastor Jonas."

"Knight family... how are you doing on this lovely Sunday morning?" he asked.

"We're a wreck. We're about to send our baby girl off to a Third World Country. Where is everyone else?" my mom asked.

"Everyone should be on the plane already. I stepped away to go to the bathroom. They were all sitting here when I left. Miss Pryce is the last to join us. You have everything you need?" he asked me.

"Yes, Pastor," I answered.

"Good. Well, I'm going to get on the plane. Gregory... Blaize... you have nothing to worry about. Your little girl is in good hands," he promised, shaking their hands as he walked away. I turned toward my parents, gave them both kisses, and said my final goodbyes. Of course, my mother shed a few tears and didn't want to let me go.

"Come on, baby. She's going to miss her flight," my father coaxed as he tried to release her grip from around my neck.

"I'll be okay, mom. It's only three weeks," I said as I picked up my carry on and started walking to the gate. Once I was checked in, I turned and waved bye to the both of them. Then, I turned and made my way on to the plane.

I walked down the aisle of the plane, looking for my seat. It didn't take me long to find it once I spotted Pastor Jonas. I walked to where he was sitting and then shimmied myself into my window seat.

"Pryce," he greeted me as I sat down. I turned toward him.

"Kevin," I said, returning his greeting.

"I had no idea you were such a good liar."

"Me either," he responded, reaching in and placing a gentle kiss on my lips.

"I don't think I've ever seen you outside of your suit and tie."

"You like what you see?"

"I sure do," I responded, pulling him in for another kiss. Like I said, I wasn't really going to Africa. Kevin and I were going to Houston so that we could spend some personal time together without having to sneak around. Kevin and I had been messing around for a little over a year. He was my first everything; my first kiss, my first boyfriend, and my first *first*. He was three times my age. He was forty-eight years old, and I was sixteen which didn't matter to me, because age was nothing but a number. You couldn't help who you fall in with. What sucked the most was that he was already married to another woman.

Kevin was my best friend, Jo's, dad. She knew I had a boyfriend, but she had no idea who he was, because I never shared his identity. I knew she wouldn't approve of it.

Kevin put this whole trip together. He printed out the application my parents needed to fill out for this fake missionary trip. He paid for the tickets and made sure we got the tickets with the layover in Houston where we would be staying for the next three weeks. Kevin and I had only had sex once, and that was my first time. We had sex in the balcony of the church on the floor. He had set it up really nice with a blanket on the floor, candles, chocolate covered strawberries, and a bottle of wine. I wouldn't have wanted my first time any other way.

"You ready to get this vacation started?" he asked.

"More than you know," I answered. He put his hand on my bare thigh as he reached over and kissed me once again. I felt his hand roam further up my thigh and under my skirt until he was tracing the laced part of my underwear. He looked at me as he bit down on his lip. He reminded me of Morris Chestnut with his dark chocolate skin tone and his bald head.

"I can't wait until I get you to that hotel," he said, rubbing his finger across my cheek.

"I can't wait either," I admitted.

KAYLEE

I looked myself over in the full-length mirror, taking in the bruises that covered the lower half of my body. I knew if I was going to go to my parents' house, I had to wear pants. When Jean and I got to our hotel room last night, the first thing Jean Claude did when we got in was deliver a punch to my ribs. It hurt, but because I was so used to the abuse, I was numb to the pain. I sat on the bed, holding on to my side as he started removing his belt. He tried to get me to admit that I'd had sex with Enzo, but I denied that shit. I wasn't about to admit to it, because I knew how bad the beating could have gotten.

I wrapped myself in a towel and left out the bathroom. Jean Claude was sitting on the bed going through his phone. Our luggage was on the bed. I walked over to mine and started digging through my clothes, looking for some pants. I thanked God that I had packed a pair of jeans. Back in Paris, I wore dresses every day, so that's all I really had in my wardrobe.

"Are you going to come with me to my parents' house?" I asked him as I started getting dressed.

"No, and you aren't either. We're going home."

"What? I didn't even get a chance to spend time with my parents," I whined.

"Oh well. You should have been doing that instead of fucking that black nigger."

"Jean, I didn't have sex with him. I swear," I lied.

"Well, if you didn't, then maybe you should have. That'll be the last time you see him. This will be your last trip here."

"What? You can't tell me I can't come see my family," I argued.

"Once we're married I can. Now, pack up your shit. We're leaving!" he yelled.

"Please, I want to go spend some time with my family," I begged.

"Fine... you want to spend time with your family? Show me how bad you want it. Kiss my ass, and I'll let you go spend today with ya family."

He stood up and walked over to me.

"You wanna see your family that bad, then kiss my ass."

"Excuse me?" I asked, looking at him like he had just lost his damn mind.

"You heard me. Show me how bad you wanna see your family," he repeated, turning around and undoing his pants until they fell to his ankles. He was now standing in his boxer briefs.

"I will not kiss ya ass, Jean. Have you lost your mind?"

"Fine... pack ya shit, and let's go," he said, pulling his pants back up, but I grabbed hold and prevented him from pulling them up. I dropped down to my knees as he let his pants fall. I pulled down his boxers, revealing is hairy pale ass. I puckered my lips as he put his hands on his knees. I pressed my lips against his ass, placing a kiss on his left cheek.

"I didn't say my ass cheeks. I said my ass," he said, spreading his cheeks as he remained in his bent position. I looked at his hairy ass crack and couldn't believe that I was about to subject myself to such behavior.

Once again, I puckered up and kissed inside his ass crack. I picked myself up off the floor along with leaving my dignity right there. I ran into the bathroom, shutting the door behind me. I leaned against the bathroom door as I wiped a tear from my cheek that had escaped my eyes. I ran over to the sink and washed my face. I dried it off with a towel and looked in the mirror before I turned away. I couldn't look at myself. I was too ashamed at what I had let this man do to me.

I walked back out into the room and put on my shoes. I grabbed my pocketbook and keys and left out the hotel room. I couldn't stand to be in this room with him any longer. He was going back to Paris by his damn self. I scurried out the hotel and hopped in the rental car, making my way to my parents' house.

It was around noon when I walked into the house. The smell of bacon filled the air as soon as I walked in. My mom must've been cooking brunch which mean I was just in time. I hadn't had some of my mom's cooking in so long. I missed it.

"Hello," I called, kicking my shoes off at the door. I walked through the house toward the kitchen. I walked passed the bathroom and almost died. I guess the bacon scent traveled over whatever the hell this smell was coming from the bathroom.

"We're in here," my mom called. I walked into the kitchen, pinching my nose closed. My mom, dad, and Bryce and KJ were sitting in the kitchen.

"Who the hell was in the bathroom?" I asked.

"Ya stinking ass brother," my father answered.

"Oh my God, Bryce."

"Nope... wasn't me," he interjected.

"KJ? I expected this from Bryce. You need a lesson in shit taking 101, lil' bro. You shit and flush, dude. It smells like somebody crawled in your butt and died."

"Shut up before I throw you in the bathroom and lock the door."

"Please don't. I'm not ready to die," I said, walking over to my mom and kissing her on the cheek.

"That's from all them fiber and protein shakes... got his ass smelling rotten," my dad mentioned. I laughed, kissed my dad, and then sat down in the empty chair next to him.

"I got here just in time. I missed your food, mom."

"You wouldn't miss it if you came to see us more often."

"I know, mom. I be so busy. You know Paris is the true fashion capital of the world. It's work, non-stop," I explained, shoving some of my mom's homemade French toast in my mouth. They were mouth-watering good. I couldn't stop stuffing my face. I knew I was gon' have to hit the gym hard after this meal.

"Slowdown, baby girl. There's a lot more where that came from," my dad said.

"How was Pryce when you dropped her off at the airport?" I asked.

"She was good... almost anxious to get on that plane. It was your mother who was crying like a damn baby."

"Aww. She'll be fine, mom. It's only for three weeks. Get rid of those two boneheads, and you'll have the place all to yourself."

"Whoa, I ain't going nowhere, 'cause there won't be none of that going on around here," Bryce spoke.

"Word," KJ said.

"It's gon' be whatever the hell I say going on in here. Now if me and my wife wanna get it in, we gon' get it in. How you think you got here?" my dad asked Bryce, making me laugh.

"My mind isn't too grown to still believe that a stork dropped me off at the doorstep."

"Yep... dropped you right on your damn head. Anyway, how long are you and the fiancé staying in Jersey?" he asked.

"Umm, I'm not sure. I think he's actually ready to go, but I'm not, so I might just send him on his way," I responded.

"Well, it would be nice if you stayed a little while longer. We could have a girl's day. I just wish my baby was here too," my mom said before she started crying. I looked over at my dad, and my brothers and KJ and I laughed quietly while my dad and Bryce just shook their head. I guess they were over it.

After I ate, I walked around the house, admiring my mother's interior decorating skills. She had the entire house decorated in gold and white. They could do that because they had no little kids running around anymore.

"What you looking around for? You looking for something to steal?" KJ asked as he came walking down the hallway. He looked like the six-foot version of my mom. Anyone outside the family would have mistaken him as being older than Bryce when, in fact, Bryce and Pryce were older than him. KJ played on the high school basketball team. Between him and Mega, they kept the family in the stands cheering. One of them, if not both, were bound to make it in the pros.

"Mind your business, monkey. Where you on your way to?"

"To the gym. Can't let Mega take all the scholarships."

"I know that's right, baby bro. Go do your thing. I'm rooting for you."

"Aight, you gon' be here when I get back?" he asked me.

"I should."

"Aight, I'll catch you later," he said, running down the stairs.

I walked across the hall to Bryce's room and peeked in. He had it set up like a music studio. He was sitting there working on some music.

"What's that you're working on?" I asked, going in and sitting on his bed.

"Just some blends I'm putting together for a party I'm DJing next week. If you're still here, you should come through and watch ya little brother work," he said. I smiled at him. My little brother was so handsome. Although he and Pryce were twins, they looked nothing alike. Pryce looked like a mix of my mom and dad while Bryce and I resembled my father.

"I'll try my best to be there, little brother. Make sure you're being productive with your life and not out here being a little man whore... like your cousins."

"Don't play my cousins out. They like having options, and although I have goals it doesn't mean I'm not running through the ladies," he responded.

"Yeah... whatever, nugget head. Let me hear something."

"Alright, I got something for you," he said, turning around and pressing some buttons. Teedra Moses's "Be Your Girl" came on. This was one of my favorite songs. I played this song a lot when I was messing with Enzo. Bryce started mixing it with some other beats, and it sounded mad dope. Lil' bro had skills.

I was sitting on the bed listening to the song, and I felt his phone vibrating. He was so busy in his computer that he wasn't paying attention. I looked down at the vibrating phone, and a guy's picture popped up... a very handsome guy whose eyebrows was arched better than mine. He didn't have a name. He just had a one eye-winking face emoji with the tongue sticking out. Something was telling me that I wasn't supposed to be seeing this, but I wanted to know if what I was assuming was true. I picked up the phone, stood up, and walked over to him. I tapped his shoulder, and he turned around to his ringing phone. He grabbed it out of my hand and turned down the music.

"Kay, it's not what you're thinking," he said with a shaky voice.

"What is it that you think I'm thinking?" I asked him.

"I'm not gay."

"Okay, Bryce. I'm not judging you. I swear... but you know if you ever need someone to talk to, you can talk to me. I'm your big sister. Your secrets are safe with me."

He got up and walked around me to the bedroom door. He looked out into the hallway and then shut his room door. He came back over to his chair and sat down, instructing me to do the same.

"I'm not gay. I'm bisexual... I think. I love being with girls, but there's this one guy that I enjoy being with as well."

"I'm guessing that guy is the cutie that popped up on your screen."

"Yeah, that's Marco. He's cool, but he wants us to be a couple, and I'm not in it like that. I'm cool with what we do behind closed doors, but I'm not ready to make it public, and I'm not ready to give up my girls."

"Does Marco know you're still involved with women too?"

"Yeah, he knows."

"So just be honest with him. Let him know you're not ready and wanna remain low key for now. If he cares for you, he'll understand."

"You right, sis. Thanks. Keep this between us, please."

"Of course. Your secret is safe with me, lil' bro," I said, rubbing his back. He went back to mixing his songs, and I sat there listening for a little while before I left out his room. I stopped in Pryce's room and started looking around. I didn't get a chance to speak to her before she left. I was hoping to get a sense of who she was by looking around her room.

Her room was remarkably clean. There was barely anything in here but her bedroom furniture, a few books, and some pictures of her friends, family, and one with her Pastor. I sat on her bed and laid back on her pillow. I put my hand under the pillow to plump it up under my head, and I felt something under the pillow. I removed it from under the pillow and looked at it.

"What?" I asked myself out loud as I looked at the Victoria Secret tag of a satin baby doll lingerie set that she had paid sixty-four dollars for.

"Lil' sis getting sexy for somebody," I spoke softly.

"Hey, baby. What you doing in here?" my mom asked from the door.

"Nothing... just checking out little sis's room. She is freakishly clean," I said as I slid the tag into the pocket of my jeans. I'm sure my parents didn't know Pryce was buying lingerie.

"Yeah, she cleans like she did a bid in the pen or in military school or something."

"I wonder what my old room looks like?" I said as we walked out of Pryce's bedroom.

"It's exactly the way you left it. No one goes in there."

I walked to my room and opened the door. She wasn't kidding. It was exactly the way I had left it. Clothes were on the bed, dressers drawers were practically open, and the blankets were pulled back.

"Dang, ain't nobody tried to help me out and straighten up a little for me?" I asked.

"We ain't make this mess, so why should we clean it?"

"Touché,"

I looked around, admiring my own taste in decorating. My room consisted of a Queen sized Victorian inspired canopy bed with the matching mirror and dresser and white carpeting. My dad had paid a pretty penny for my bedroom set. I knew how to get my way with him. I would hold my breath until I was blue in the face, and he'd just give in and give me what I wanted. I had been doing that since I was nine.

I walked around, picking up clothes and looking at them. I think it was about to time for me to go through some of these clothes and give some to Pryce and Ruby. They were really nice and expensive clothes and shoes. I'm sure Pryce would love them. She'd been after my clothes since she was ten years old.

"I remember when I bought you that shirt," my mom said about the silk button up shirt that I had in my hand.

"Yeah, I'm thinking about giving it to Pryce."

"She would love it. So, what's going on with you and Jean Claude?" she asked.

"Nothing, why you ask that?"

"I just picked up that vibe yesterday. Plus... you're here, and he's not."

"Everything is fine with us, mama. He just wanted to relax back at the hotel, and I wanted to spend time with you guys."

"Okay, if you say so, but you know what they say... a mother always knows."

I wasn't beat to continue this conversation with my mother anymore. She had the ability to pull things out of you that you didn't want to be said. I continued to straighten up the room while she talked. Bryce coming out of his room caused her to stop talking, thank God.

"Hey, baby boy. Where you on your way to?" she asked him. He walked into the room to see what we were doing.

"Damn, I haven't seen the inside of this room since the last time you were here. Shit still a mess," he joked.

"Shut up, big head. One of y'all could have cleaned it for me."

"We ain't make the mess, so why should we have cleaned?"

"Same thing I said, son."

"Whatever," I responded.

"Where you off to?" my mom asked once again.

"I have to run somewhere real quick."

"Where... to one of them little fast little girl's houses?"

"Nah, ma. I'm going to the store," he answered, coming in the room and kissing my mom on the cheek. Before leaving out of the room, he deliberately knocked the pile of clothes I had on the bed back on to the floor.

"Aight... when you come home, your whole room gon' be flipped upside down!" I yelled. Although I was annoyed at what he had just done, I had to admit that I missed times like these; overbearing mom, annoying little brother, little sister with secrets, and a father who just stayed out of it all. We were the traditional family.

"Be safe, buckle your seatbelt, and make sure you strap up. I don't want to hear you crying because it burns when you pee again!" my mom yelled down the hallway to Bryce, and I fell out laughing.

"Ma, for real?" he asked, embarrassed.

"Sorry, go on... have fun," she said and waved. She turned to me and started laughing.

"That was so wrong, ma."

"It was, but it was funny. What you want to do today?" she asked me.

"Whatever you want... I got all day."

"How about we get your dad's credit card and go to the spa to get a mani and pedi?"

A spa trip sounded great and much needed, but then I remembered the marks and scars on my legs that I knew would be exposed if I went to a spa.

"How about a mani, pedi, and we sneak some tacos into the movies like old times," I suggested.

"Sounds like a plan. You finish up here, and I'm going to go coerce your father's credit card out of his wallet."

"Go do your thing, sis," I said as she left the room. I opened my underwear drawer and started straightening it up so that it could close. After removing all of the underwear out the drawer, I noticed the picture that was sitting at the bottom. I picked it up and sat down on the floor to look at the picture. It was a picture I took of myself and Enzo a few years ago. We were laying in his bed when I took this picture. His face was pressed into the crook of my neck. We had fun that night. We ordered some Pizza Hut, played some games, and watched some Netflix and chilled. I missed the times we had together. Although we were sneaking around back then, we'd made some beautiful memories together.

I ran my fingers over his face. I could still remember how he smelled that night. I brought the picture to my chest as I pulled out my phone. I scrolled through my phone's contact list until I reached Enzo's number that was stored under Edith. This was a different phone, so when I converted from my old phone to this phone, something wouldn't let me delete his number.

I pressed dial and placed the phone to my ear. The phone rang for a while until his voice resonated through the phone. He said hello about three times before I decided to speak.

"Hey, Enzo. It's Kaylee."

"Hold on," he said. I suddenly became nervous, and I didn't know why. I'd just had sex with this man in the bathroom yesterday. I didn't know why the sound of his voice just made me nervous.

"My bad... I have Malachi here helping me with something, I had to leave the room. What's up, Kaylee?" he asked. His voice caused my body shiver.

"Nothing, I was just thinking about you and wanted to give you a call."

"Really?" he asked. I could hear a smile form through his voice.

"Yes, I found a picture of us and started reminiscing. You were so perfect, Enzo."

"I still am, Kaylee. Nothing changed about me."

"Yeah... well, a lot has changed about me, and I'm not proud of it. Can I see you later?" I asked.

"You sure that's a good idea? I'm not blind, Kaylee. I saw that mark around your neck yesterday."

"It was nothing. I broke out from a necklace. It left a bad rash on my neck," I explained. After he left out the bathroom and I looked in the mirror, my sweat had managed to slightly wipe away my makeup. I noticed it once I looked in the bathroom mirror. I wondered to myself if he had seen it, and I guess he did. I adjusted my scarf before I went back outside so that no one else would notice it.

"Where's hubby?" he asked.

"Back at the hotel."

"Malachi and I gonna be at the daycare until about six. I can come pick you up after," he suggested.

"Can we make it around seven? I'm supposed to be spending today with my mom."

"Aight, see you then."

I hung up the phone and stood up off the floor. I looked at the picture one more time before I placed it on to my mirror instead of hiding it in the drawer. I finished cleaning up my bedroom and left out, shutting the door.

LIL' RUBY

*A*fter I ate breakfast earlier, I went back upstairs and went back to sleep. I woke up around 1:30 pm, showered, and got dressed in a pair of jean shorts, a tank top, and my combat boots. Yesterday morning, I went to the Dominicans and got a blowout, so before I went to bed, I wrapped it up so that it wouldn't mess up. I had long natural hair that I got from my mama. Once I combed it down, it dropped to the middle of my back. I sprayed some of my Vaseline moisturizer on to shine these legs up.

I could hear Mega's TV going, so I knew he was home. I looked down the long hallway to where my parents' bedroom was, and their bedroom door was open, so I knew they were either downstairs or weren't here.

I walked down the stairs, heading to the kitchen to grab a Gatorade out the fridge. I heard the back door slide open, and I turned around.

"Oh… hey, Ruby. I didn't know you were home. I only saw your dad's car parked in the driveway," Genesis explained. I stood there, taking in her appearance. This bitch was damn near naked standing in my kitchen. She had on a netted see-through bathing suit cover and bikini bottoms on with no bikini top. The sight of her nipples was clear as day.

"You thought my father was in here, yet you still waltz ya ass in here half naked?" I asked, pointing to her ensemble.

"I'm sure he's seen titties before, Ruby. It's not a big deal."

"It's a big deal to me. You're disrespecting my mother and her house."

"Whatever, little girl," she said, lifting her hand up and turning around, about to walk out the door.

"Let me tell you something," I said, walking up to her.

"You bring yo' ass in this house like that again, I'll cut ya nipples off and shove them down your throat. Try me if you want, hoe. Best believe my brother will be hearing about this."

She rolled her eyes and then turned and walked out the house. I watched as Genesis walked back across the yard to the guest house. I couldn't wait until the day I got to smack this bitch.

I grabbed a banana out the fruit bowl, got my keys off the counter top, and left out the house.

I pulled up on Auburn and parked in front of my girl, Harmony's, house. She lived directly across the street from Jayon's building. I looked up at the building from my car, wondering if he was dead. I knew his bedroom window had a fire escape, so it was a possibility of him making it out alive. Either way, I didn't care. I should have just burned his dick off.

I got out of the car and walked up on to her porch where she was sitting with her Peach-a-Rita and her peach Amsterdam bottle. At nineteen, home girl was a damn alcoholic. She drank more than most adults I knew. Every now and then, I would drink a Peach-a-Rita with her, but that was it.

"What up, trick?" I greeted.

"What up, crazy chick?" she responded.

"Why I gotta be all that?"

"Because you are a fucking lunatic. I know yo' ass did that to Jayon's apartment."

She laughed.

"You know nothing. I ain't do shit. Where my cousin?" I asked her, talking about Trey. Trey and Harmony had been messing around for some time now. Although Harmony was nineteen, she was very mature for her age. Trey was nine years older than Harmony, but he took care of her every need as well as the needs of their child. They had a two-year-old son together. I was the only one in the family that knew about Trey's son because no one really stayed connected with Trey but me. He made me promise not to tell anyone else. They didn't like that he sold drugs, and when they gave him the ultimatum, he chose the streets. What the family didn't know was that Trey had a baby on the way at the time, so he needed to do what he needed to make sure his son was good.

Trey was like a son to my parents. They would have been ecstatic to learn of Trey's baby. They would have helped him take care of the baby until he was able to find a legit job. It shouldn't have been hard, because Trey had his bachelor's degree in computer science from St. Peter's University in Jersey City. My parents paid his way through college, so imagine their disappointment when they found out he was letting his degree go to waste to sell drugs.

Trey was really good with computers. He could hack anybody's computer and get their bank account information or any other personal information that he shouldn't have had access to. I tried to talk him into hacking my high school computers to give me an A in all my classes so that I didn't have to show up and actually do the tedious school work. He wouldn't do it. He wanted me to finish school the right way. I didn't see the purpose... seeing as though I knew more than the dumbass teachers in that school.

"I don't know where he went. He jumped in the car and sped off like twenty minutes ago. He was pissed about something," Harmony explained.

"He's always pissed about something. If he would have just stayed his ass home with us, he wouldn't have a reason to be pissed all the time."

We sat there chilling for a little while before Harmony pointed across the street. I looked over, and Jayon was walking toward me. I sat back on the steps and waited for him to come over here with the drama. When he finally reached the porch, he just stood there looking at me.

"What... you just gon' stand there, or you gon' speak your mind?" I asked.

"You could have killed me, Ruby," he finally spoke.

"And?"

"What you mean *and*? All my shit was destroyed."

"So. Did flappy tits burn along with the rest of your stuff?" I asked.

"Flappy tits?" Harmony asked.

"Yep, he was fucking some bitch with some *do your titties hang low* bitch."

"What?"

"You tell me. Do her titties hang low? Do they wobble to and fro? Can you tie 'em in a knot? Can you tie 'em in a bow? Can you throw them over your shoulder like a continental soldier?" I asked.

"Shut the fuck up, Ruby. The only reason I fucked her is because yo' ass holding the fuck out. I'm a man, Ruby. I have needs that you were neglecting."

"If you thought for a second I was gon' give you my virginity after you've cheated on me numerous times, you done bumped your damn head. You are definitely not worth it. I gave you chance after chance to prove yourself, and you still fucked around on me. You take flappy tits, and go on about your business."

"You lucky I don't go tell the cops that it was yo' ass that set that fire," he threatened.

"You ain't stupid, motherfucker."

"Fuck you, Ruby."

"Never!" I yelled in a joking manner as he walked away, mad. Harmony and I laughed.

"You's a fool," she said.

"Forget his black ashy ass."

I grabbed one of her Peach-a-Ritas and cracked it open. Half a can of this usually got me drunk. I wasn't much of a drinker. Every now and then, I would grab a beer from the fridge just to piss my dad off, but I never intended to drink them.

We continued to chill on her porch by ourselves until Trey showed up like an hour later with a blunt in his hand. He had a scowl on his face, and I was curious to know what the hell was wrong with him now. If you asked me, Trey resembled the rapper Big Sean. He even had his style. My cousin was really handsome, but he was mean as hell... not to me but to other people. He adored me. Hell, everyone adored me.

The baby started crying, so Harmony ran upstairs, leaving Trey and I sitting on the porch.

"What's up with you?" I asked him, reaching for the blunt. He smacked my hand away. I sucked my teeth. He never allowed me to smoke around him, but when Harmony and I were alone, I smoked every now and then.

"That nigga, Polo, who I had doing the runs for me got popped for weed. Good thing that nigga ain't have that work on him when he was pulled over. I had to ride over there and get that shit from his crib. I gotta find someone to run this shit up to Connecticut."

"Let me do it."

"Shut the hell up, Ruby. You done lost your damn mind. I'll find someone else to do it. What's been going on at the house?" he asked.

"Same ol', same ol'. I'm trying to get rid of that bitch, Genesis."

He laughed.

"What she up to?"

"Being a skank like always. That bitch trying to hit on my father. I'm gon' have to slice that hoe up."

"Leave that girl alone, Rub," he said, taking a pull from his blunt.

"Eww, why you taking up for her?" I asked, confused.

"You're supposed to be on my side, remember?"

"I'm always on your side, baby girl. You know that. Let me go check on them," he said, walking in the house and up the stairs.

I sat outside on the porch for a few minutes before I started hearing moaning and shit coming from inside Harmony and Trey's apartment.

"Oh my God. Eww."

I picked up my keys and phone and hopped in my car. I'd talk to that bitch later and make sure I cursed her ass out too. She could have given me a warning or something. I pulled off and drove in no particular direction. I had nowhere to go. I would usually go chill with Jayon, but I wasn't fucking with him anymore, so I decided to go chill with Jace. I knew he would be doing something exciting.

Hopefully, he'd let me take the four-wheeler out. I been trying to drive that shit for the longest. He was stingy with it. My cousin, Jace, resembled Monty, the rapper from Remy Boys. He had the coolest little patch of grey hair in the center of his head just like Pryce and Aunt Tiffany, but theirs were in the front of their heads. That was like a family trait of theirs. Nico didn't have the patch. His grey hairs were spread throughout his whole head. It still looked nice on him though.

I got to Jace's house, and I heard the music and the sound of engines revving up. My adrenaline started pumping. I walked around to the back of the house, but I saw no one. I was expecting a backyard full of people. I walked into the garage.

"Here's where the party at!" I yelled over the sounds of the engine. Jace poked his head out from under the hood of the car.

"What's up, lil' cuz?" Jace greeted, walking over and kissing me on the cheek.

"What you doing here?" he asked.

"I was bored, and I knew you would be doing something fun."

He laughed as he went back under the hood of a nice ass Cadillac Escalade. It was probably a stolen car he was about to start stripping.

"Who is this?" a voice asked coming from around the truck. His looks immediately piqued my interest. He had light brown shoulder-length dreads, beautiful hazel eyes, and one of those mini beards. He had to be about six feet two, 180 pounds, and he had to be in his mid to late twenties.

"I'm Ruby. Who you?" I asked him.

"I'm Chop," he answered, walking closer to me. He smelled like Cocoa Vaseline and men's Degree deodorant. He smelled clean, and I liked it. I think I was in love.

"Nice to meet you, Chop," I said, shaking his strong hand.

"Same, sweet thing."

"Whoa. Chill, son," Jace said, coming from under the hood of the car again.

"Why chill? This your shorty?"

"Nigga, I know you just heard me call her lil' cuz."

"Don't listen to him. He's inhaled too many of these car fumes," I said, making Chop laugh.

"How old are you?" Chop asked me, looking my body over, and I was enjoying every minute of being under his glare.

"I'm eighteen," I answered.

"Nice... are you going to ask how old I am?"

"I don't really care," I answered. He laughed.

"Yo, J, do you mind if I take your beautiful little cousin outside and have a conversation?

"Hell yeah, I mind, nigga."

"Aight... good lookin'," he said, ignoring Jace and leading me outside to the backyard. We sat in the two lawn chairs that were outside.

"Ruby? You don't look like a Ruby."

"Well, my real name is Diavion, but my family calls me lil' Ruby after my great grandmother."

"Diavion. Can I call you Baby D?" he asked.

"You can call me whatever the hell you want."

"I like that," he responded with a laugh.

As he was talking, I couldn't stop staring at his thick pink lips. They made everything he was saying sexy. He could call me a bitch, and I wouldn't have even been offended. I wondered what those lips would feel like pressed against my lips, and I wasn't talking about the ones on my face.

"Is it possible for me to take you out one day?"

"If it's not, I will damn sure make it possible."

"Cool. If I ain't know no better, I would think somebody had a crush."

"You thought right. I know I said I didn't care, but how old are you?" I asked.

"I'm thirty, ma."

"Wow, you don't look a day over twenty-five."

"Is my age going to be a problem?" he asked.

"Not with me. With my parents, maybe, but they don't need to know."

"I like your style, Baby D. I might have to make you my little shorty."

"You do what you gotta do, boo."

As we sat there talking, all I could think about was how his mouth would taste. It looked like it tasted like strawberry lemonade. He was doing most of the talking while I sat there staring into his beautiful eyes. I caught some things he was saying, like the fact that he had a ten-year-old daughter. I really didn't care. She better get ready to call me step mommy because her father and I were about to get married.

We sat out there talking until Jace's blocking ass came out there interrupting us. He and Chop had to be somewhere, so Chop and I exchanged numbers, and he told me he would hit me up later. I walked away, smiling from ear to ear and leaving my cousin, Jace, blowing steam from his ears.

I was really feeling Chop. Jace boosted cars for Chop, and Chop paid him out of pocket. That meant Chop had money, and I liked a money-making nigga. I didn't care how he made it ... long as he made it.

I jumped in my car and pulled off, heading home. I typically wouldn't have been home this early, but I was going home to wait for my phone call from Chop. I felt like a teenage girl with a high school crush. Oh, wait... I was a teenage girl, but this was no high school crush.

MALACHI

got home around 7:30, and my mother was pulling me right back out the door. I was tired. I just wanted to shower, lay my ass down, and maybe give Rhyes a call, but my mother had other plans for me.

"Where are we going?" I asked her as we walked out to the garage where she had a van waiting for us. I looked in the back, and Beauty and Beast were both back there.

"On our date," she answered, walking around to the driver's side of the van. I got in the passenger side and put my seatbelt on.

"Ma, where are we going?" I asked her again.

"Somewhere... just sit back and relax," she insisted. I did exactly that. I laid my head back in the seat and closed my eyes. The sound of heavy breathing in my left ear caused me to jump up.

"How can I sit back and relax with your mutt breathing down my neck?"

"She likes you. If she didn't, she would have bit your ear off."

I shook my head and pulled my seat up to get as far away from the dogs as possible. My phone started vibrating, and I removed it from my pocket. It was Trey.

"What up, cuz?" I answered.

"Shit, what you up to? You wanna hit up Mr. G's?" he asked.

"Nah, I'm on my way somewhere with moms."

"Who is that?" my mother asked.

"Trey," I answered. She made a face.

"Hey, Trey," she greeted him.

"Hey, ma. How you doing?" he asked her.

"I'm good... missing your face. You ready to come home?" she asked him. Although my mom gave him the ultimatum, I knew deep down she really didn't want him to choose to go.

"Nah, ma, I'm doing good. I swear. I have someone I want y'all to meet."

Although Trey was estranged from the family, it didn't mean we loved him any less. My mom raised him like her son. They had a bond, but just like she gave him the ultimatum, she would give her kids the same.

"Uh oh. Let me guess... you got some girl pregnant, and you're about to be a father," my mom guessed. The other end of the phone got quiet.

"Nah, she's not pregnant. I do have a boy. He's two years old," Trey informed her. The news caused my mom to hit the brakes so hard that I felt one of the dogs hit the back of my seat followed by an *Arr* sound. I started laughing.

"Oh shit! Sorry, Beauty," my mom said, reaching her arm back and consoling her dog. She took the phone from me.

"You're telling me you have a two-year-old son, and you're just now telling me? I could break your neck right now, Treon."

"I know, ma. I wasn't sure how you were going to react. Y'all did kick me out. I didn't think that y'all would care."

"Excuse me? We didn't kick you out. You chose to leave. You bring that baby to see me first thing tomorrow."

"Aight, ma, I'll bring him tomorrow," he agreed.

"You better. Here," she said, slamming the phone into my chest. I slid it into my pocket.

"I can't believe that boy."

"So, I met Rhyes today," I said, changing the subject.

"Yeah, I sent her to the daycare," my mom said.

"Why you ain't been introduced me to her? Baby girl got it going on."

"Yeah, she's a good girl. I thought you and Genesis were a thing."

"We are... but not a forever thing. Rhyes... she's popping," I said, thinking about her face.

"I think you two would look nice together. Did you get her number?" my mother asked with a smile.

"You know I did. She was a little nervous about giving it to me because she didn't know how you would take it."

"Rhyes is one of my favorites. I don't have a problem with the two of you at all. Now, if she hurt you, then I'm gon' have to hurt her."

"How can she hurt me, ma?" I asked.

"You never know. These women today are some scheming little bitches. They can make the strongest man cry. I'm not a scheming bitch, but I made your father cry a few times. G-Ma threatened to slap my face off a couple times," she said, making me laugh. I believed her too. G-Ma was forever threatening to slap somebody. Even at the age of eighty-nine, she was still raising hell. That's why her little old self still living. They say the ones who raise the most hell lived the longest.

"G-Ma is a fool. I see why ya named lil' Ruby after her."

"Exactly, but let Rhyes know I'm fine with it. You need a girl like her in your life. She's strong, ambitious, and she has goals."

"You don't think Genesis has goals?" I questioned. My mom was good at reading people. She knew a snake when she saw one and could sense bullshit a mile away.

"I know she has goals. I think one of them is to keep it in the family. I see the way she looks at your father. I'm just waiting for home girl to make her move so that I can make it her last. The last two women that tried to get at my husband, one is somewhere with a bullet in her skull, and the other is buried in the ground with a hole dug into her chest from a really terrified and very hot rat ... or did I feed her to the hyenas? No, I think that was your grandfather or maybe your uncle JoJo. Either way, I don't play when it comes to my husband or my kids. I'll run that little heffa through a wood chipper," she said as she continued to drive. I sat in the passenger seat, mortified.

"Wait ... you're joking, right?"

"No," she answered nonchalantly. I had come to the conclusion that my mother was freaking deranged. How the hell did my father put up with that for almost twenty years? I guess when you take those vows with someone, no one and nothing could come between them, not even murder. My mom and pops were definitely made for each other. I remembered their wedding vows like they took them yesterday.

"With this ring, Troy, I give you my heart, my soul, and my life. I promise that from this day forward, you shall never be alone. There's no other man I would rather be three steps to the left of. It's you and me forever, baby; the queen to your king and the Bonnie to your Clyde. You got mine, and I got yours," my mom said.

"Troy, will you please repeat your vows to Camilla."

"Camilla, baby girl, my Sunshine, the light of my world ... with this ring, I give you my heart, my soul, and my life. I feel like everything that has happened in my life has led me in your direction. Your presence is the air I need to breathe. Without it, I may as well die. I love you for all the things you've done for me and to me. You accepted my son as your son without a question, and I respect you for that. You are beautiful inside and out, and you're strong and the true definition of a Queen. You got mine, and I got yours forever, Sunshine," Troy said, with tears now streaming down his face.

My parents' love was epic. I think it was about time they renewed their vows. I think I was going to set that up.

We had finally gotten off the highway in Newark and pulled up to a gate. My mother pressed a button inside the van and the gates slid open. We pulled inside the crowed parking lot. My mom pulled up to the front and parked directly in front of the door.

"What is this place?" I asked my mother as we exited the car.

"This is a place that your daddy and I own," she answered.

"What kind of place?"

"It's just an empty space that I occupy every now and then to make some extra money. You'll see once you get inside."

She opened up the door to the back of the van. Beauty and Beast started going crazy. They must've known where they were.

"Calm," my mom spoke softly, and the both of them calmed down immediately.

"Beast," she called and then backed up from the van. Beast jumped out the van and walked up to my mother. I never really took in how big he actually was. If he stood on his hind legs, he probably stood taller than me. He was indeed a beast. His coat was all black, and his muscles bulged out his body like he was on steroids or some shit.

He stopped walking and stood in front of my mom.

"Beauty," she called, and Beauty jumped out the van. She was slightly smaller than Beast, but she was still big as hell too. She had a marble brown and black coat, and she had the weirdest green eyes. She walked over to the left of Beast and sat down.

"Good girl. A Queen always stands to left of her King. Three steps behind is the most powerful position for a Queen," she said, bending down and kissing Beauty on the top of her head.

"Where did you get that from? I remember you saying that in your vows."

"It was Jada Pinkett Smith's homage to Will. She said a queen's most powerful position is to the left of her king three steps behind. Anything that comes toward him from behind, she'll encounter first. She can clearly see what advances to his right and his left. She also has sight on what approaches ahead. If a queen stands beside her man, she can only focus on what's ahead, and if he swings his sword, she'll be struck. Three steps behind is the most powerful position for a queen."

I nodded my head as I thought about what she had just said. It made a lot of sense, and her vows finally made sense.

"You ready?" she asked.

"Ready for what?"

"You'll see."

She smiled and turn to walk away. We walked up to the door, and my mom put in a code. It was the date she miscarried the baby after Ruby and before Mega. That was her go-to passcode for a lot of her accounts and keypads everywhere. That was one of the saddest times of her life.

We walked in the building and down the stairs. The building was quiet which was odd because there were so many cars outside. We got down the stairs and, once again, my mom put in a code. The doors came open, and we were bombarded by noise; yelling, screaming, and dogs barking. This door must've been sound proof because outside was quiet as a fucking mouse.

"Alright, alright, alright! The queen is here!" someone shouted over a microphone. My mom and her dogs walked in and into the middle of the room. A bunch of niggas and their dogs lined the side. I walked in the middle of the room and stood next to my mother. I looked around, and it was set up like a stadium. There were people sitting in bleachers, holding up signs like they were at a game. Behind us was a four-foot-high, ten feet by ten feet chain link gate set up.

My mom was handed a microphone.

"How is everyone tonight? Y'all ready to make some money?" she asked, and they all started hooting and hollering.

"Or lose some money, depending on who you bid on. I can tell by some of these signs I'm seeing that a lot of you are probably going home broke," she joked, and the crowd laughed.

"This here," she said, grabbing me by my cheeks.

"This is my prince, my son, Malachi. He's here for the first time, so I want y'all to help me show him a good time, okay? Let's get this show on the road. Give me Ruger. Give me Rampage," she requested with a wave of her hand. The two owners walked their dogs to the middle of the room where we stood. They were brought buckets of warm water and both started wiping their dogs down. When they were done, they walked their dogs one by one into the gate, standing on opposite sides. They were ready to get it in immediately.

My mother started walking back to the sideline, and I followed her along with Beauty and Beast.

"How many of y'all rocking with Ruger?" she asked the crowd. People started screaming.

"Who rocking with Rampage the savage?"

Once again, the crowd started yelling.

"I don't know. It sounds like a tie. Ruger and Rampage, give us a show. Fight!" my mother declared. The owners removed the leashes from the dogs, and they started getting it on. The crowd started yelling and chanting as the two dogs tore each other apart. The dog, Rampage, was really giving it to Ruger. I see why they called him a savage.

"Why do they have to wipe down their dogs?" I asked my mother.

"Because owners have been known to rub their dog down with oils to prevent the opponent's bites from sticking."

"Damn, it's that serious?"

"You have no idea how serious these people take this. Some men train their dogs like boxers, making them run treadmills, and isolating them from society. It's serious. It be a lot of money on the line. A dog owner can leave here with up to four grand a fight. That's a lot of money to some people."

"Damn, four grand a fight?" I asked, starting to reconsider my career choice.

"Yep, but it all depends on the crowd we can generate. Your mama here leaves out with the most. No one is allowed to place a bet lower than five hundred. Entrance fee is fifty per person. We get no less than a hundred people in here a fight. I keep the door money and ten percent of the bets. Some nights, I can make five grand. Other nights, I can make close to fifteen grand, but like I said, that depends on the crowd we can get here without getting the attention of the authorities."

"That's why Beauty and Beast so big? You fighting them?"

"No, my babies don't fight. They kill and clean up."

"Kill what?"

"Whatever I tell them too," she answered, never taking her eyes off the fight. By the end of the fight, the dog by the name of Ruger was down for the count, and Rampage the savage stood victorious.

"Maybe next time, Speed. Let's get this cleaned for our next fight."

"Ma, where's the bathroom?" I asked. She showed me where the bathroom was, and I quickly jogged off. I wanted to hurry back to see the next fight. Though the shit was fucked up, it was entertaining as hell.

The bathroom appeared empty, but then again, I really didn't take a look. I just ran over to take a piss. I heard what sounded like nails tapping on the floor. After I was finishing using the bathroom, I peeked under one of the stalls. There was someone in the stall with their dog. I washed my hands and was looking myself over in the mirror. Through the mirror, I noticed whomever it was drop what appeared to be a syringe. I turned and looked. I assumed whoever it was, was shooting up. I couldn't see the person, but he had on some Navy Blue Huaraches, and the dog had a distinguished set of paws; one white and the other grey. I shook my head and walked back out to the main room. There was a bar in the back, so I stopped and got a Henny and coke.

"So, you're the Prince," the cute bartender asked as she made my drink.

"I guess you can say that, and you're Beauty?" I asked her, going by the embezzled name on the front of her shirt.

"I'm Princess," she responded. I laughed.

"I guess we're a match made in heaven."

"I guess so."

"I'm Malachi," I said, extending my hand. This must've been my lucky day. I ran into two beautiful girls in one day and had one at home waiting on me.

Princess was a redbone, about five feet three inches, and 120 pounds. She had some cute chubby cheeks, and her eyes were slanted a little like she was mixed with some kind of Asian descent. Her hair dropped just below her shoulders and was curly. She was gorgeous. If I had to choose between who was prettier between her and Rhyes, I wouldn't be able to choose. They both were individually gorgeous. I pulled out my wallet and gave her a twenty.

"You have a man, Princess?" I asked her as she walked over to the register. I looked at her fat ass as she stood there getting my change. The ass part of her shorts was embezzled with the word Beast on it. The name Beast fit that ass perfectly.

"Yep, his name is King. Come here, baby," she said, tapping her thigh, and a little ugly ass mutt came running toward her. I couldn't even tell you the breed of the dog, because I didn't even know. The little fucker looked like he got into a fight with some clippers because he was missing patches of hair everywhere.

"What the hell is that? It looks like a reindeer fucked a Brooklyn rat, and that was the result," I said. I guess she was offended because she stood there with her mouth open.

"What? I'm serious. What breed is that?"

"I don't know. I adopted him. He was found roaming the streets in Irvington."

"I see why. Nobody wanted that ugly shit."

She started laughing.

"Stop. Leave him alone. He's sweet."

"If you say so," I said, taking a sip from my cup.

"Anybody ever told you that you look like the actor, Rotimi, from Power?" she asked. I let out a little laugh because I got that shit a lot.

"I'm cuter," I responded.

"You most definitely are."

She started wiping down the bar. I grabbed one of the dollar bills that was my change.

"Give me a pen," I said to her. She turned toward the cash register, grabbed a pen, and handed it to me. I wrote down my number on the dollar bill.

"Hit me some time," I said, handing her the bill. She smiled and bit down on her perfect bottom lip. I pulled out another twenty and placed it on top of the other bills that was supposed to be my change.

"What's that for?"

"Best Henny and Coke I've had in my life," I said and walked away toward my mother.

"You're just in time. The next fight is about to start. You trying to date all my workers?" my mother asked with a smile and rubbing my back.

"You saw that?"

70

"I see everything, baby," she said, lifting the microphone to her mouth.

"Give me Taz. Give me Cannonball," my mother requested at the same time my phone vibrated. I unlocked my phone and read the message. It was an unfamiliar number, and the message was just a crown emoji. I looked over to Princess, and she waved. I gave her a head nod and went back to watching as the owners walked their dogs in the middle of the room, started wiping them down with the warm water, and then walked them into the gate. Taz was amped up. He was damn near pulling his owner into the gate. He was ready to go. My mother gave the owners the go ahead and unleash their dogs. Taz took off toward Cannonball and had his whole face in his mouth in a matter of three seconds.

"Shit, Taz is a beast," I said to my mother.

"Yeah, he's one of the best fighting dogs in here, if not the best."

I noticed the dog, Taz's, paws. I looked at the owner's sneakers and knew they were the ones in the bathroom stalls.

"Damn, Taz acts like he be shooting up with his owner," I said out loud.

"What you talking about?" my mom asked, never taking her eyes off the fight.

"When I was in the bathroom, the dude right there was in the bathroom stall shooting up."

"What makes you think he was shooting up?" she asked, now looking at me.

"He dropped the needle."

"Did he have the dog in the bathroom with him?"

"Yeah."

"He wasn't shooting up. He was lacing his fighter."

"You mean shooting the dog up?"

"Yep. I'll deal with it."

We sat there watching the fight until the end. Taz ended up winning the match. During the match, my mother wore a scowl the whole time. She walked over to one of the men that stood guard and whispered something in his ear. He nodded his head and followed Taz and his owner. Something was about to pop off, and I was interested in seeing what was about to go down.

~

AFTER MA DUKES dismissed the crowd, we walked toward the back and into a room. Inside the room was the guard from before, Taz, the dog and his owner, and Beauty and Beast.

"Did you do it?" my mother asked the guard.

"Yeah," he said, handing her a card. She looked at it and flicked it at the dog owner.

"You cheating in my house? You know how I feel about cheaters?" she asked him.

"I didn't cheat, queen, I swear," he said with fear in his eyes. I looked over at my itty-bitty mother and tried to figure out what was so fearful about her. This nigga really stood here ready to shit his pants. I guess he knew something that I didn't know.

"That card says otherwise. Torch removed blood from Taz, and it came back positive for acid. Can you explain that?"

"I don't know, queen. Maybe it was something he ate."

"Don't lie to me, Percy. You been stealing money from me, my fighters, and my people. How long you been lacing Taz?"

"I'm not."

My mom held her head down and started pacing back and forth. My mom always knew when someone was lying. She walked in between Beauty and Beast and kneeled down between them.

"I don't like thieves, Percy."

"I didn't steal anything from you, queen."

"Do you know what happens when someone steals from their queen? Their hands get cut off," she said, walking over to her two dogs and kneeling down between the two of them. She whispered something I couldn't quite make out, but they did. Beast and Beauty both lowered their heads, and their growls echo throughout the room. I ain't gon' lie. My soul damn near escaped out my ass.

"Queen, I'm sorry. I'll pay you back every cent."

Beauty and Beast started walking toward him.

"Queen, please. No."

"Kill," she said once again, and both of the big dogs took off toward the dog, Taz, and started tearing him apart. The poor dog tried to fight back, but he was no match against one of those dogs, let alone two. The sounds coming from Taz were gut wrenching They ripped him from limb to limb until there was no more Taz.

His owner was standing there crying at what he had just witnessed. Probably his most prize possession was just ripped to shreds.

"Sorry we had to do this, but you can blame yourself. Taz was damaged goods. He was the canine version of a crackhead, and that's all your fault. It's sad. A person who loves their dog would never shoot their dog up with narcotics, because they know it ruins them neurologically. Once they serve their purpose, they must be put down, Percy. You know this," she explained.

"Fuck you, queen. Fuck you. You killed my dog, you bitch. You will pay for this."

"What, nigga?" I asked, now pissed that he was speaking to my mother in that tone. I started walking up to him, ready to knock his ass the fuck out.

"Malachi!" she called, getting my attention. I turned toward her. She was still in her kneeling position.

"Don't worry about him, baby boy. See, I was just about this close to letting you walk up outta here," she said, standing up to her feet.

"Kill," she ordered, and once again, Beauty and Beast turned toward their victim and slowly approached him as blood dripped from both of their mouths. Percy put up his hands like he was squaring up with a human. Those dogs were about to chew those fists right off. They charged him, knocking him into the wall behind him.

I sat there and watched as Beauty and Beast savagely ripped off every one of his limps. I couldn't watch anymore. I turned around toward the wall. I looked over at my mother, and she was just leaning against wall like she was watching sports or something. She wasn't bothered the least bit. Now I believed her when she said she'd fed someone to a hyena.

"Malachi, you can leave out if you want," she said.

"Nah, ma, I'm good."

She nodded her head and turned back to the dogs.

"Enough," she said, and Beauty and Beast stopped their attack. My mom really had these dogs trained. They weren't only pets to her but weapons of mass destruction. Both dogs came walking toward her.

"Let's go get you two cleaned up."

I finally turned back around, and the man by the name of Percy was no more. Not only did they kill him, they devoured him. These dogs really did eat people. That's why their asses were so big.

"Torch, you got this?" she asked him, and he nodded his head. We exited the room and walked outside. She walked around the side of the building, turned on the hose, and handed it to me.

"You hose 'em. I'll dry 'em."

"Yeah, 'cause I ain't going nowhere near their mouths."

She started laughing.

Once we were done washing them, we loaded the dogs into the van, and we pulled off. We got home around 11:30. If we were still living in our old home, we would have been home sooner. It took us about forty-five minutes to get to our Saddle River home. Our home spread across six acres. We had ten bathrooms, eight bedrooms, and two pools; one indoor and one outdoor. The guest house had five bedrooms and three bathrooms. This house was three times bigger than our last house. Trey and I moved out here once I turned eighteen. It was my mother's idea because she said she didn't want girls walking through her house.

"So, did you enjoy our date?" my mom asked me.

"Yeah, I did ... everything except watching you order someone's death," I answered.

"That's not the first time you've seen me kill someone."

"What you talking about? When was the first time?"

"When you were five, around the same time you were shot. Do you even remember that? Being shot?"

"Vividly," I answered.

"Really? You never spoke of it."

"Nothing to really speak about. I remember being shot, but what I remember the most were your screams, watching the tears fall from your chin, and the feeling of them hitting my face. I think that was more traumatizing than the actual shooting. I dreamt about that night for years."

The whole time I was talking, I was thinking back on that night my mother and father rushed me to the hospital. The sounds of my mother's cries were all coming back to me.

She reached over and ran her hand across my cheek. I grabbed her hand and kissed it.

"Good night, ma," I said, getting out the car. I opened the back door, let Beauty and Beast out, and watched as they slowly walked to their kennel with Beauty three steps behind Beast to his left.

"What's wrong, babe? I been sitting here playing with ya dick for the last thirty minutes, and you have yet to get hard," Harmony said, breaking me from my thoughts.

"Nah, it was just something I heard earlier that's just been fucking with me," I answered.

"Do you want to talk about it?" she asked.

"Nah, I'm cool."

"Don't play me, Trey. I know you, and I know when you got some shit on your mind. Now spill it," she demanded, sitting up in the bed. I looked up at her and sat up in the bed with her.

"I was on the phone with Malachi earlier, talking to him and my aunt Camilla. I guess they thought they hung up the phone, but they didn't. I overheard my aunt admitting to killing my father and grandfather," I revealed.

"What? Are you sure that's what you heard?" she asked.

"I'm certain that's what I heard."

"Do you think your aunt is capable of something like that? You sure she wasn't just talking?"

"My aunt don't say shit just to be talking. Besides her lying about

76

how my father died, she has always kept it a hunnit with us all. She has never lied to me or my cousin a day in my life, so I believe it."

"Damn, baby. I'm sorry about that. What are you going to do?"

"I don't know, but if it is true, and something deep down inside is telling me that it is true, somebody is going to pay, family or not."

"Besides your aunt and uncle, do you have any other relatives that you can talk to?" Harmony asked. I really had to think about it because it was so long ago since I'd come to live with my aunt and uncle.

"My dad had a friend named Porter. I haven't seen him since I was eight years old. I don't know if he's still around or not."

"Do you remember where he lived?"

"Yeah. He lived right next door to my grandfather's old house in Irvington," I answered.

"Well maybe you should go talk to him. Your father may have told him something about your uncle."

"Yeah, maybe. That's if he still lives there. I'm gon' go have a chat with cuz too. I told them I would bring lil' Trey by so that they could meet him."

"I don't know. I don't know if I want my son around your family," Harmony expressed.

"He'll be fine. Besides the suspense about my father and grandfather, they're actually caring fucking people. They could have let my ass go to foster care, but they took me in and gave me a great home and amazing fucking life. I'm starting to think that was all out of guilt for killing my only living relatives."

"I'm sure you think they're caring people, but like I said, I'm not sure if I want my son around them."

I sat back in the bed, thinking about the last time I'd seen my dad, and I couldn't remember. It seemed like so long ago when I went to stay with my aunt and uncle. I don't even remember what my father looked like but I remembered my grandfather. He was the one who took care of me. My father was too busy running the streets to even give me a bath. I never knew my mother. I wasn't ever sure if I had one. I mean, I knew I had one, but I felt like I'd been living with my dad and granddad since I was baby. I didn't even know her name. I'm sure Porter knew her. I might ask him about her too. I was going to go have a talk with him tomorrow. I just hoped he still lived in the same spot.

~

THE NEXT MORNING, I got up out of bed and dropped my little man off at daycare. After I dropped him off, I went and did some running around before I went to Irvington to see about Porter. I pulled up on my old block and drove through slowly. Everything around here looked exactly the same, even my old house. I pulled up in front of the house that used to be Porter's. I got out the car and started walking up to the house.

"Can I help you?" someone asked as I walked up to the bottom step. I looked up, and there was an older man standing on the porch. He looked familiar but not quite.

"Yeah, what's up? I'm looking for Porter," I responded.

"Why you looking for Porter?" he questioned, looking down the stairs at me.

"He knows my pops."

"I know a lot of people's pops. Who yours?

"JoJo."

His demeanor changed. He started walking down the steps to where I stood. I backed up because he was getting a little too close.

"Lil' Trey," he said with a smile and extended his hand so that we should shake hands.

"I don't know how I didn't recognize you, son. After all, I am your god father."

"Word?"

"Yeah. Your pops was my best fucking friend. Come on. Come inside. I can't believe this shit."

We walked into his house. It was a little messy but decent. He pointed to the love seat and told me to have a seat.

"I can't believe this shit ... JoJo's boy. I swear I never thought I would see you again. I had no idea where you had gone," he said, sitting across from me in a recliner.

"That's what I'm here to talk to you about. After my pops died, I went and stayed with some family. I believe they had something to do with his death."

"Troy?" he asked, cracking open a can of Budweiser.

"You want one?"

"Nah, I'm good, and yeah, my uncle Troy. He and his wife took me in."

Porter nodded his head and took a sip from his can.

"Your father was a low-down bastard. He was selfish as all hell. That nigga would do anything for money and wouldn't care who he hurt to get it. As we were growing up, he drove your grandfather fucking nuts. I almost felt bad for your grandfather, but your grandfather never gave up on that father of yours, and your father knew it. He took advantage of everyone, including me, but ya pops was my nigga. Your father was shitty. When your grandfather found out about Troy, JoJo was so jealous that it was scary. Your father kidnapped Troy's boy for ten grand ... his own flesh and blood. Your father wasn't right, but your uncle Troy wasn't right either. He had some enemies in these streets. They ever told you how they're able to live that lavish life?" he asked. I shook my head no.

"Word is that he kills people for a living. He's a paid hitman. That wife of his has more enemies than he does. Now that's one crazy bitch. She kills people for the fun of it. I know someone who works security for her. He said she's into some ruthless shit."

"I overheard her admit to killing my father and grandfather and some shit about feeding them to hyenas or burning a hole through their chest or some shit like that. Do you think she's capable, or is she just smoking shit?"

"I don't know, son. Like I said, these are just stories I'm hearing, but from those stories, I wouldn't put it past her. Maybe you need to go talk to them."

"They'll probably just lie about it."

I continued to talk to him, catching up with him. He said he wanted to meet lil' Trey. I told him I would bring him by one day when I had the time.

After I left him, I planned to go talk to my aunt and uncle, but not today. I wasn't going to stop until I found out the truth.

KAYLEE

I woke up the next morning to a beautiful purple sky. I inhaled the summer breeze that entered through the cracked window and had brushed across my face. It felt like I was inhaling a breath of life. I had never felt so alive in the last three years than I did now.

Last night after Enzo got off, I volunteered to meet him here at his place. My mom and I hadn't come back from our girl's day by the time he had gotten off. When we got back to my parent's house, I said my goodbyes, jumped in my rental, and drove over to Enzo's house. When I got there, it felt like old times with me and him.

We had ordered some Pizza Hut and watched movies. He had turned into some kind of health freak, so the only snacks he had were some veggie chips, Greek yogurt, and granola bars. He even made sure the pizza had veggies on it. I didn't mind though. I was trying to watch my figure anyway.

I looked at the clock, and it was five in the morning. I rolled over toward him. He opened his eyes and was staring back at me.

"I think I should be getting back to my parents' house before they come looking for me," I said, gently touching his right cheek.

"Don't worry about him. If he don't know where you are, he can't take you back," he said, wrapping his arm around my waist.

"Yeah, well I also don't want to put my parents in the middle of this."

"Don't leave now," he begged, crawling between my legs and kissing me on the neck. He placed trails of kisses down my neck and down to my belly button, making his way down to my naked waxed vagina. I grabbed on to the back of his head as he proceeded to nibble and suck at my vagina like he was eating a plum. He definitely knew his way around my body.

All night long, he made love to my body like it belonged to him. He knew my ins and outs and all my spots. After three long years, he was still an expert on my body. Last night, he made me forget about the last three miserable years with Jean Claude.

"Mmm, Enzo," I moaned as I held on to his head, pushing his face further inside my wet spot. He reached his hands up and started stimulating my nipples, making me even wetter than I already was.

"You want me to stop?" he asked, coming up for air.

"Not yet," I answered. He smiled and went back down.

"Just keep doing exactly what you're doing, baby."

I rotated my hips as I held on to his head. He moved his tongue in and out of my hole, scooping up all of my juices as they flowed. After five minutes, he was turning me on my stomach. He kissed the back of my legs and then bit down on my right ass cheek and then placed a kiss directly in the spot he had just bit. He ran his tongue between my ass cheeks and up my back until he was nibbling on my ear.

"You know I still love you, Kaylee, right?" he whispered in my ear.

"Yes, I know. I love you too, E," I responded.

"So then stay with me."

"Please don't ruin the moment, baby. Just keep loving me, please."

He said nothing else. He responded by pushing his hard penis inside my delicate flower. It was still a little tender from the pounding he had put on me last night.

"You okay?" he asked, responding to me jumping from the slight pain.

"Mmm hmm."

He placed his hand in front of my body as he started rubbing my clit while he pushed in and out of me.

After five minutes I was reaching my climax. I took over and started rubbing at my own clit as he held on to my waist. He was at his peak as well.

"Leave it in or pull it out?" he asked. He had me so turned out at this point that I wasn't thinking clearly, so much so that I told him to leave it in.

"You sure?" he asked. I never answered him. I just concentrated on reaching my climax.

"Shit, Kay. I'm about to nut."

"Come on then," I encouraged. His moans and groans grew louder, and his thrusts grew wilder. Before I knew it, my orgasm had taken over my body, sending me into seizure-like convulsions, and his movements seized. We both laid there exhausted, fighting to catch our breaths.

~

IT WAS around six when I crept into my parents' house. I removed my shoes at the door and started walking up the spiral stairs. I was so busy concentrating on the way I was walking that I ended up walking into someone coming down the stairs. I looked up to an unfamiliar female face.

"Oh shit, sis. You just getting in?" KJ whispered from behind the unfamiliar female. He had on basketball shorts and no shirt, and the female, who looked to be older than I, had on a little mini dress with her shoes in her hand and her hair all over the place. KJ must've snuck her in after our parents went to bed.

"Yeah, but the question is what the hell you think you doing?" I asked with my hands on my hips, trying not to be too loud and wake my parents who would be getting up any minute.

"We were studying."

"Studying, my ass. She looks like she could be your teacher. You better get her out of here before Mom and Dad wake up. I'm going to bed," I said, walking past them. I crept down the hallway as quietly as I possible until I got to my old bedroom and shut the door. I started stripping down into nothing but my underwear and Enzo's wife beater tank top. I crawled in bed and nuzzled under the covers. My mom must've known I was going to be sleeping here because the sheets on the bed were changed. I figured I would get a little sleep and shower before I went back to the hotel. I was planning to tell Jean that he could leave, and I was staying here.

～

I WOKE up feeling relaxed and refreshed like I belonged in a Summer's Eve commercial. I stretched my limbs out across the king size bed like a starfish. It had been a while since I'd slept in a bed alone or even woke up without being afraid of being laid back out by a punch or slap to the face. I looked at the time, and it was ten in the morning. I hadn't slept passed eight since I graduated college.

I turned around and sat up in the bed. I felt a stinging pain to left side of my cheek that laid me back down onto the plush pillows. I sat back up quickly to see Jean Claude sitting at the edge of the bed. He had one hell of a reach.

"What are you doing here?" I asked him as I massaged my stinging cheek.

"You think you have the right to question me? Where the fuck were you, and why didn't you come back to the hotel?"

"Because I wanted to stay with my family, Jean, not in no damn hotel. You can take yo' ass back to Paris, but I'm not going," I stated, taking my big ass engagement ring off my finger and tossing it across the bed at him. I climbed out the other side of the bed, closer to the door. I grabbed for the doorknob and opened the door a little when it was slammed shut by Jean Claude.

"Whose shirt do you have on?"

"Mine, now get off of me."

"You take this bullshit off and put on some appropriate clothes so that we can get out of here," he demanded, pulling at the shirt.

"Get your hands off of me. I'm tired of your shit, Jean Claude. You get your disrespectful ass out of my parents' house.

"I'm not going anywhere without you, bitch."

He seethed as he backed me into the wall behind the door.

"You belong to me," he spoke through gritted teeth with the most devilish look in his eyes.

"Not anymore. I belong to no one but me."

He raised his hand about to strike me, but he was deterred by a knock at the door.

"Is everything alright in there?" my mom asked from the other side of the door.

"Yes, mom. Jean Claude was just leaving."

"Okay. There's breakfast, if you two are hungry."

"Thanks, mom. I'll be down in a second."

"Alright."

I pushed Jean Claude away from me, but he didn't move much. He towered me by at least six inches and overpowered me by forty pounds.

"Move out of my damn way."

He looked down on me as he slowly moved out my way. I walked into my walk-in closet and flipped on the light. I started looking for something to wear. Some of the clothes I had in here I would have never been caught dead in back in Paris. I decided on a Nautica navy blue and lavender tie dye maxi dress that still had tags on it and some silver Steve Madden open toe sandals that tied up the leg. I removed the dress from the hanger and popped the tags.

I removed Enzo's T-shirt and was standing there in nothing but my underwear. I heard the closet door shut, and I looked over to the door where Jean Claude stood.

"What are you doing?" I asked him. He started unbuttoning his button up shirt and then removed it as he started to unbuckle his belt.

"I want you to leave," I said, backing up further into the closet until I

85

couldn't go anymore. He came closer to me, grabbing me by my hair and swinging me into another wall where he grabbed me by the neck and squeezed as hard as he could. While choking me, he lifted me up into the air where my feet were now dangling. He ripped my underwear off with his free hand and dropped his own pants. He loosened his grip around my neck. I used my hands to claw at his face, but he kept moving.

"Get off me!" I shouted. I knew even if I screamed that no one would hear me. Bryce locked me in here for a whole day once, and no matter how loud I yelled for someone to come let me out, they never heard me. Bryce came later on that night and finally let me out. He had to be around twelve or thirteen around that time, little fucker.

"Like I told you. You belong to me," he said as he pried my legs open and inserted his fingers into me.

"You wanna tell me you didn't fuck him now, you little whore."

He removed his fingers and wiped them across my face. He then grabbed on to his pale white dick and shoved it into me. I tried fighting him off of me, but the harder I fault, the tighter his grip became around my neck and the harder he slammed into me.

"You belong to me. You hear me?"

He pulled himself out of me and slammed me down to the carpeted floor. I tried to use that to my advantage to get up, but he kicked me back down.

"Lay your ass back down. You didn't have a problem lying on your back for that nigga."

He laid back on top of me and enter me once again. He grabbed my leg and lift it up, giving himself better access as he pounded inside of me.

Once again, I tried fighting him off, but it wasn't working. He was stronger than I was. I couldn't believe what was happening. *Was I really being raped? Could I even consider this rape, being that he was my fiancé?* I fought more and more until I became exhausted and gave up. I could tell he was getting off from the fight I was giving, so I stopped and just let him finish.

"You let that nigger loosen you up for me, right? I can feel it. Your pussy isn't as tight as usual."

He kept pounding, harder and harder until he was coming inside of me. He laid there on top of me, catching his breath as I just laid there with my head to the side, unable to look at him. I just wanted him off me and out of my sight. A few minutes later, he stood his feet and started fixing his clothes as he looked down at me. He buttoned his shirt and tightened his belt around his waist. He grabbed one of my shirts that were hanging in the closet next to him and wiped the sweat from his forehead. I sat up and leaned against the wall. He pulled something out his pocket and dropped it on the floor in front of me. Then, he turned and walked toward the closet door.

"I'm going back to the hotel. I'll be catching the first plane out of this wretched country. I'll leave your things in the hotel. When you're ready to act right, you know where I'll be," he voiced as walked out the closet, leaving me on the floor. I looked down at what he had taken out his pocket, and, it was my ring. I kicked at it pushing it into the back of the closet as I began to cry.

After a few minutes, I got up off the floor, grabbed my dress, and walked out of the closet. I needed to clean myself of him. I grabbed a pair of underwear from my drawer. I peeked outside the door to make sure that there was no one to see me in such disarray. The coast was clear, so I quickly stepped out my room and made a dash to the bathroom, shutting the door behind me and locking it. As I was in the shower, I let the warm water beat down on my skin. I ran my hair through the water without any care as to how it would look when it dried. My hair wasn't like my mom's and Pryce's. Once they wet their hair, it curled up beautifully. I had that hair that got nappy once it was wet. Thank God for length because I was able to pull it to the top of my head into a cute bun.

I got out the shower and got dressed. With a little Spanish gel, I made do with my hair. I left out of the bathroom and walked to the top of the stairs

"MA, CAN I USE SOME OF YOUR LOTION?" I yelled down the stairs. My dad appeared at the bottom of the stairs.

"Now typically, I would complain about you yelling in my house like that, but I actually missed your voice, baby girl … just like old times," my dad said with a smile.

"Aww! Thanks, dad, and I miss causing havoc around here. MA!" I yelled again.

"Oh my God, Kay. Look inside my bathroom," she finally answered. I smiled down at dad.

"Twenty-six, and I still got it."

I ran into my parent's gigantic ass room. This shit was like something you saw on *MTV Cribs*, the Beyoncé and Jay-Z edition. I walked into the bathroom and grabbed my mom's skin moisturizer. She got her moisturizers custom blended to her liking. She paid like sixty dollars a bottle for this stuff and her body wash. It was definitely worth it. It left your skin tingling with a cooling sensation.

When I was done getting dressed, I walked down the stairs into the living room where my dad sat watching TV.

"Hey, dad," I greeted as I walked toward the kitchen.

"Hey, baby girl."

He returned the greeting, never looking away from the television. I walked into the kitchen where my mom was sitting at the table with her Kindle. I reached down and kissed her on the cheek.

"Your food is in the oven."

I walked over to the oven, grabbed the mitts, removed the plate from the oven, and sat it on the table.

"What you reading?" I asked as I walked over to the fridge and poured a glass of orange juice."

"*Stay* by Ivy Simone."

"How is it?"

"Let's just say watch out for egg shells in your breakfast. I couldn't put this book down, so I was cooking and reading at the same time," she answered, never taking her eyes off the Kindle.

I sat down at the table and started eating my food. Between my mom reading and me stuffing my face, the kitchen was quiet. Something told me to look up, and I did. My mom was staring at me over her Kindle.

"Ma, what?" I asked. She put down her Kindle and continued to stare at me, freaking me out.

"Where were you last night?" she asked.

"What you mean? I was in the bed sleeping," I answered.

"You may have been in a bed sleeping, but it wasn't yours, and it wasn't the hotel bed that you and your fiancé shared seeing as though he came here early in the morning looking for you."

"I don't know what you're talking about, ma. I was sleeping in my bed."

"I heard your door close at six this morning. I'm a mother. I have ears like a blind bat. I hear everything. Don't lie to me, baby."

"I was with Enzo," I admitted. She looked at me with a stern look then looked away from me.

"Is that the reason you're not wearing your engagement ring?"

"No. Enzo is not the reason why I'm not wearing my ring. The reason I'm not wearing the ring is because I've been unhappy in my relationship, and Enzo reminds me that love should be glorious, and love shouldn't hurt."

"What you mean *hurt*?" my mother said, gently placing her Kindle down on table.

"Emotionally, mom."

"Oh ... well you know you can't find the answers by jumping in the bed with another man."

"In some instances, you can't, but in my situation, I did. I love Enzo. I always have. I love Jean too, but he doesn't make me feel the way Enzo does. He never has. Plus, I miss home, and I miss my family. I don't want to go back to Paris, and Jean Claude isn't willing to move to the States. I'm sure I can find a job out in the city. "

"Just like that, huh? You have everything planned out?"

"No, I'm still planning things out, but I'm staying home. I'm not going back to Paris. I'll go back to get some of my things, but that's it."

After what happened upstairs just now, I was sure that I was done with Jean Claude. He would not get the satisfaction of thinking that he owned me. I was nobody's property but my own.

"Okay, baby. It has been nice having you back home. Should I start calling Enzo my new son in law?" my mom asked.

"No, not yet. We're still rekindling."

I smiled. I finished eating my breakfast and decided to go see my girl, Octavia. I hoped she still lived in the same spot as before because I had no other way of getting in touch with her.

MALACHI

$\mathcal{I}$ woke up the next morning for work tired as fuck. I was able to sleep in later because I had no morning classes. The seventh and eighth graders had a trip today, and those were my morning students. I looked over at Genesis who was still sleeping and then looked over at the clock. I removed my little man from my shorts and rolled over to Genesis, pulling her panties just below her ass. I knew she wasn't sleep, because as I was pulling her panties down, I felt her slightly lift up so that I could get them down a little more. Her ass wasn't slick, trying to play sleep. I placed my fingers on my tongue, gathering a little saliva so that I could moisten my dick to slide right in the pussy. When I was in, I grabbed her shoulder with one and her waist with the other and started slamming my pelvis into her ass, giving her every inch of this dick. About seven minutes later, I was pulling out, spilling my nut onto her ass.

I rolled out the bed and walked into the bathroom. I wet a cloth and then walked back to the bedroom to clean her ass off. I went and jumped in the shower so that I could get ready for work. After washing my ass, I did everything else I needed to do before walking out the bathroom.

"Who the fuck is Rice, and why do you have her number?" she

asked, holding up the pink sticky notes that had Rhyes name and number on it.

"None of your business, and why the hell you going through my pockets?" I asked.

"Because I can. You lucky I don't know the password to that damn phone."

"No, you lucky you don't have the passcode. It's some shit in there that'll hurt ya little feelings, girl," I said, going to sit down on the bed with my back facing her as I rubbed lotion into my skin.

"What kind of name is Rice anyway? You fucking with some Asian bitch?"

"What, Genesis? You sound fucking stupid. Her name is Rhyes, and she's just a shorty I met the other day."

"Oh yeah. We'll see how you get in contact with that bitch," she said, ripping up the sticky note and then walking out the room. I laughed to myself. She could rip that paper up all she wanted. I knew where I could find her and get it again.

I heard the toilet flush, and she came stomping back into the room. I paid her ass no mind as I continued to get dress.

"You trying to play me out, Malachi? If that's the case, then I can just get to stepping," she insisted.

"You do what you gotta do, baby girl. Maybe it's a good thing. Save yourself," I said.

"What's that supposed to mean?" she asked.

"Meaning, if my mother caught you eyeing her husband again, she was going to cut ya fucking eyes out and feed them to her dogs. You think we blind? You think I don't see you eye-fucking my Pops? Ruby told me about your little stunt yesterday, walking into my mom's house half naked and shit. You disrespectful as hell, and I don't want that shit around me."

"What? Ruby doesn't know what she's talking about."

I laughed. This bitch was crazy. One thing was that Ruby always knew what she was talking about. Lil' sis didn't have a perfect GPA for no reason.

"Don't disrespect my sister. She saw your shit from the very beginning, but I needed to see the shit myself before I dropped ya ass. That night I came in and my father's picture was in your phone, I knew right then and there that you had to go."

"But I told you that I was just deleting the picture," she whined.

"Yeah whatever. Just make sure you have your shit gone by the time I get home from work."

I finished buttoning up my shirt and sprayed some cologne on. I checked myself out, making sure I looked professional enough to walk into the school building. I couldn't wait until I got there so that I could take this shit off and put on my gym gear and sneakers. They had a rule in the school that every teacher must look presentable upon walking in the school, but once inside, I was able to change.

"Oh, and leave the key on the table when you leave," I said before walking out of the house. I left her standing there with her mouth open. At least I was able to get a farewell nut.

~

"You don't know how to duck, little man?" I asked one of my sixth graders, Roy. I had the class playing dodge ball, and he stood there and watched as the ball came straight at his face. I don't know what he thought was going to happen as he stood there watching it. Maybe he thought he could stop it with his eyes. I was crying deep down inside as the scene of him getting hit played over and over again in my head. I couldn't laugh out loud with the rest of the class, because I had to play the concerned authority figure.

I held his nose with tissue, waiting for it to stop bleeding.

"I didn't see the ball," he said.

"You need glasses" I told him because there was no way he couldn't see a bright ass neon green ball coming toward his face.

"I don't know. Maybe."

"That wasn't a question, kid. I was telling you that you need glasses. Maybe we'll have the nurse give you an eye exam."

"Okay," he said. I removed the tissue from his face, and it appeared the bleeding had stopped. I cleaned him up and made sure he sat down the rest of the gym period and future gym periods until he got his vision checked.

After I dismissed the class, I had to do an injury report and call his parents. I pulled up his records in the school's system and came across his parents' names and number. This couldn't be a coincidence, but at the same time, it was a big ass coincidence.

Rhyes Harris.

There was no way in hell that there were two people walking around with that name spelled the same way. I picked up the phone and dialed the number that was on the screen in front of me.

"Hello," she answered. I sat quietly, trying to figure out if this was her voice.

"Hello," she said again. I heard a bunch of babies and kids in the background. It was definitely her.

"I don't know, girl. I think the stars are trying to tell us something."

"Excuse me. Who's calling?" she asked.

"This is Malachi, or shall I say, Mr. Jones, calling from P.S. 19."

"Oh … hey, Malachi. How are you?" she greeted.

"I'm doing pretty good, and yourself?"

"A little confused. Why are you calling from P.S 19?" she asked.

"I'm Roy's gym teacher. He got injured during a game of dodgeball. It's protocol to call the parent after an injury."

"Oh my God. Is he okay?" she asked with concern in her voice.

"Yeah, your kid is good. He just had a little nose bleed, but he's good."

"Thank God. I didn't know you were a gym teacher."

"I didn't know you had a kid."

"That's because you barely know me, Malachi, and he's not my kid. He's my little brother. I have custody of him."

"Cool. Have you had lunch yet?" I asked her. The phone got quiet.

"I don't usually take a lunch. I use my lunch break to go pick my brother up from school at three and bring him here."

"Well, I'll bring lunch to you. How about that?" I asked. She took a while to answer.

"Ummm, okay. That'll be fine."

94

"Good. Either way, I was still coming. What do you have a taste for?"

"Whatever. Surprise me."

I laughed.

"I'll be there in an hour, okay?"

"See you then," she said, hanging up the phone. I removed the phone from my ear as I sat back in my chair, thinking about the big ass coincidence. How ironic is that the kid that got injured under my watch turned out to be the kid brother of the girl that I was feeling?

~

AN HOUR LATER, I was pulling up to the daycare in my 2017 Audi S7. I noticed Enzo's work truck was out here as well as my mom's Range, so I got out and went in to see what was up. I got out the car and walked into the building.

"Hi, can I help you?" the lady at the front desk asked.

"Yeah. I'm Malachi, Camilla's son. Is she here?"

"Oh yeah. Those pictures do you no justice. You're finer in person."

I laughed.

"She's in back."

She pointed toward the back where the classrooms were. It was a little quiet, so I'm guessing it was nap time for the little ones. I heard talking coming from one of the classrooms, so I followed the sound of the voices. I peeked my head into the class, and there were about six or seven women in there, including my mom and Rhyes. There were also platters of sandwiches on the table.

I cleared my throat, getting everyone's attention.

"Dammmmnn, who is that?" I heard someone whisper like they weren't going to be heard in a quiet room. My mom turned around.

"Hey, baby," she said, walking over and giving me a hug. I looked over at Rhyes and smiled. She smiled back.

"You hungry?" my mother asked.

"Nah, I got food in the car," I answered her, never taking my eyes off the beautiful woman. My mother followed my eyes over to Rhyes.

"Uh huh, that's why you weren't eating ... talking about you on a diet," my mother said, putting Rhyes on blast.

"Here I was, thinking you came in to see me," she continued.

"But I am on a diet," Rhyes said with a smile.

"I came here to bring this beautiful woman here some lunch, but I came inside to see you, beautiful Queen," I said, kissing my mom's hand.

"You are a smooth talker just like your father."

I winked at my mom.

"You ready?" I asked Rhyes.

"Yeah, just give me a second," she said.

"Aight. I'll wait for you up front."

I left out the room and went to find Enzo. He was in Rhyes's new office. I looked around, and he was damn near done. He was just painting the inside of the office.

"What up, bro?" I asked, causing him to turn around.

"What's up, nigga?" he returned, giving me dap.

"This shit looks good, man."

"Thanks. I should be done by today. Then your girl could have her office after the paint dries."

"Are you even supposed to be painting with the kids in here?"

"Ya moms dropped a pretty penny to get the odorless quick drying paint. Those brats will be fine."

"Cool."

"What you doing here? Came to see your moms?" he asked.

"Nah, came to get Rhyes."

"Ah shit. Lunch date?"

"Yeah, you know a little something. I went and picked up some food so that we could sit and eat."

"My nigga."

"I'm ready," Rhyes said from behind me.

"It looks really nice in here, Enzo. Great job," she complimented E.

"Thanks. Enjoy your lunch."

I gave Enzo a pound as I turned and watch Rhyes while she walked down the narrow hallway. That knee length dress she had on was hugging her body in all the right places. I was dying to see what she looked like outside of those clothes that were soon to come.

I ran ahead of her and held the door open so that she could walk out, and I led her to my car where I opened the car door, allowing her to get in. I walked around to the driver's side and got in.

"Before I feed you, I must tell you that you look beautiful today. I wish they had workers like you when I was in daycare."

"Shit, I wish I had a gym teacher like you when I was school. Maybe I wouldn't have had to do gym over in summer school," she said, making me laugh. I reached in the back and grabbed the pizza boxes, bringing them to the front.

"Pizza. I love me some pizza."

"Oh yeah. I thought you were on a diet."

"I am, but you're worth breaking my diet."

"Good to know."

"So tell me something, Malachi. How does a gym teacher afford a $70,000 car?" she asked.

"First off, I'm impressed that you know the market value for this car, and if you must know my parents have a savings fund for all of us that we can cash out once we graduate college. I chose to buy a car with mine."

"You are such a man," she said, making me laugh. My parents placed a hundred grand in an account with each of our names on it, and once we graduated college, we were able to do what we wanted with it. That was like a little motivation for us to finish school. Trey received his as well. He did the smart thing and invested his money. My father was surprised and proud of him at the same time. He was expecting Trey to do something reckless with the money. That goes to show how well my father actually knew his nephew. Trey was always talking about investing money and all that Wall Street stock market shit. He had dreams and aspirations. He just got involved with the wrong crowd.

"What would you have done with the money?" I questioned. I was eager to hear her answer. Her answer would give me a hint as to what kind of person she really was.

"Well for starters, I would get my brother out of public school, no offense. Then, I would give my mom a beautiful headstone, and with the rest of the money, I would put some aside for both of my siblings."

"You wouldn't do anything for yourself?"

"Doing for them is doing for myself."

"You're big on family?"

"I am, although I don't have much of it. It's just me, my brother, and I have a sixteen-year-old sister. My sister barely comes home. She has chosen to run the streets. She comes home every now and then. The path she's going down scares me. Those two are all I have. My mother died in a motor vehicle accident eleven years ago. She was pregnant with my brother at the time. The three of us were given to my father who was never really in our lives in the first place, and when we were given to him, we barely saw him then. He was a drunk who came around like every two months when I was younger, gave me five dollars, and walked along side of me while I rode my bike to Eastside Park. I don't know what my mom was thinking, getting pregnant by him more than once. I'd been taking care of my brother and sister since I was thirteen. They were all the family I had. I would like a big family of my own one day."

"Yeah, me too. I already have a big family."

"Do you have any kids?" she asked me.

"I have a two-year-old daughter in Minnesota with her mom. She'll be here in two weeks. She's coming to stay the summer with me."

"Really? That's awesome. I would have never expected you to have a kid. You don't look like the kid having type."

"What's the kid having type?" I asked, wanting to know what she meant by that.

"I don't know. You know how you look at some people and be like, *he look like he got about twelve kids*? I look at you and see a Playboy but a responsible Playboy."

"A responsible Playboy," I repeated with laughter.

"I like to have my fun."

"So is that what I am? Someone you can have fun with?" she asked, taking a sip from her drink.

"No, I like you. I want to see what you're about. I like what I see so far, and my mom speaks highly of you, so that's a plus."

"Someone vouched for me. Who's going to vouch for you? How I know you won't waste my time?"

"I vouch for me. You've just got to give me the chance to prove that I'm worth more than just you breaking your diet. Take a chance on me, baby. Let me show you a good time."

"Alright, you do that. I like to have fun too."

"Hopefully not my kind of fun.

"Your kind of fun meaning being a Man whore?" she asked.

"Yeah, something like that," I admitted. We finished eating our lunch, and I walked her back inside the daycare.

"Can I hit you up later?" I asked as I stood in front of her and looked down into her bright brown eyes. They were the color of chestnut. She had a cute mole that decorated her brown face just above her lip.

"You do that handsome," she said, standing on her tippy toes and pecking me on the lips. I smiled.

"I look forward to more of those in the future. Enjoy the rest of your day, beautiful."

I got back into my car and drove back to the school. I was ready to get this day over with. I wondered if Genesis got all her shit out yet. I was expecting a fight from her, and I was going to give her one. Even if I had to get her shit out myself, she was getting out one way or another.

I got back to the school around 1:30. I had two more classes before my work day was over and my night life began. I felt my phone vibrate in my pocket. I removed it and looked at the screen.

Princess: Good Afternoon, Malachi.

I smiled. I was having one good ass day.

Me: What's up, Princess?

Princess: Not much, I wanted to see if you wanted to come chill with me later on tonight.

It didn't take me long to decide what I wanted to do. I already knew when I saw her number pop up on my screen that I wanted to see her.

Me: Sure thing, baby girl. Just send me your address. I can be there by eight if that's ok with you.

Princess: See you then.

I put my phone back in my pocket and ran to the middle of the gym floor to organize a game of kick ball.

LIL' RUBY

"One more week of his bullshit, and then I'm out, bitches," I gloated as I walked out the school with my entourage following behind me. Nina and Raven were friends of mine, but I wouldn't consider them best friends. I didn't really have any best friends, just acquaintances.

"Miss Jones, Miss Valez, I hope the two of you have your speeches ready," Principal Skylar voiced from behind us. I rolled my eyes. I couldn't stand this silicone stuffed skank. Principal Skylar wasn't your average principal. She was young, about thirty-five, she dressed inappropriately for her job, and she openly flirted with students. There were rumors circulating about her messing with a few of the students here. That bitch was a whole hoe on the low.

"I got these ready for you," I responded.

"Excuse me," she asked.

"Oh, I said I got a speech ready for you."

I was the Valedictorian, and Nina was the Salutatorian. We had the highest grade point averages throughout the entire school, so we were required to make speeches at the graduation. I don't know what the hell they were thinking about allowing me to make a speech. I was about to turn that motherfucking graduation the fuck out.

"Okay, I can't wait to hear it. Have a good night, ladies," she said as she sashayed to her Lexus.

"That bitch is a joke."

"Your parents still letting you have the graduation party at your place?"

"They ain't letting me do anything. I do what the hell I want," I lied.

"Yeah. Okay, Ruby. You keep telling yourself that. I saw your mom, and she is scary but sweet at the same time. I don't know how that is even possible.

"My mom is cool. She's only scary when you get on her bad side, and I'm forever getting on her bad side."

I sat on the hood of my car as I continued to talk to these two chicks. I had two different sets of friends. I had my hood friends, and I had my school friends. My parents weren't too fond of my hood friends, but they never minded my school friends coming over.

"You study for the finals?" Raven asked.

"Fuck no. I'll just wing it like I always do," I answered. The sound of a motorcycle caught my attention. I looked up as a black and red Honda motorcycle that pulled into the school's parking lot and stopped across from where we were sitting. I couldn't see under the dark helmet, but after taking a good look at the driver's physique and the dreads that hung out the back of the helmet, I knew exactly who it was. A smile parted my lips. He removed his helmet and smiled back at me.

"Who the hell is that?" Nina asked with her face twisted up.

"One of God's most beautiful creations."

He reached around and unhooked a helmet from the side of his bike.

"I'll see you skeezers later," I said, jumping down from the hood of my car. I threw my book bag inside my car and locked it up. I walked across the street to Chop, grabbed the helmet from him, placed it on my head, and hopped on the back of the bike. Chop slowly pulled off until he got to the street, and that's when he took off down the block. He hopped on the highway, and we sped in and out of traffic. My adrenaline was pumping, and I wasn't even the one driving, but I wanted to. I think I had found my graduation present from my dad.

Behind me, I heard police sirens. I turned around, and there was one pulling up behind us at full speed.

"Oh shit," I said and turned back around, holding on to his waist tighter. Thank God I did because Chop took off faster than before. I didn't think he could go any faster. The cop car behind us tried keeping up, but there was no damn way he was catching up to us. I had to admit that this was probably the most fun I'd had in some time. I turned around and watched as the cop tried it's hardest to keep up. I gave the cop a middle finger as Chop got lost in traffic. He weaved in and out of the rush hour traffic on Interstate 17.

Minutes later, we were pulling into the parking lot of Wendy's. He parked his bike behind a truck, and we hopped off. He removed his helmet, and I did the same. I don't know what came over me, but I walked up to him and kissed him hard on the lips. I backed away.

"My bad. I think it's the adrenaline," I admitted. He smiled and grabbed me by the back of the neck, continuing to kiss me. He stuck his tongue in my mouth and our tongues tangled in each other's mouths. His mouth tasted like Big Red. I could suck on his tongue forever. He backed away.

"I just felt like kissing you."

"Cool with me."

"Come on. Let's go get something eat."

"Wow, this a cheap ass first date," I joked.

"This ain't a date. This is just two friends splitting a four-for-four."

I laughed.

"What? I can't even get my own meal? Shit, you cheap."

"What's the fun in having our own meal? Sharing is more intimate. The more you get to know me, you'll see that I value intimacy."

"A street nigga like you values intimacy. That's rare."

"I'm not your average nigga, Baby D," he said, draping his arm over my shoulders as we walked into the restaurant. We got up to the counter, and he really ordered one four-for-four meal. We sat down and split it between the both of us.

"So where's your boyfriend, Baby D?" he asked.

"What makes you think I have a boyfriend?" I said, answering his question with a question.

"A beautiful girl like yourself? You should have someone claiming you."

"I did a few days ago, but I caught him with a chick with long ass titties, so I set his apartment on fire," I told him as I stuffed a fry in my mouth. He laughed.

"You fucking with me, right?" he asked.

"Nope. I set it on fire and gorilla glued the door shut."

"Creative. Did he get out?"

"Unfortunately, yes. He was able to escape."

He just nodded his head and then took a sip of the strawberry lemonade.

"I know next time to make sure the windows are glued shut too."

"Next time? You think there's going to be a next time?" he asked, sitting back in his seat and looking at me.

"Yep, once you're my man."

He laughed.

"I'm sure you got women throwing coochie at you left and right, and I'm sure it'll be tempting for you."

"I'm a one woman man, baby. If you're my lady, then you're my only."

"I'm pretty sure that's what all men say."

"I'm not all men."

"I'm a virgin, kinda," I admitted. He released a little laugh as he continued to play with a piece of paper he had in his hand.

"What you mean kinda? Either you're a virgin, or you not."

"I've had a few people go down on me, but that's it. I've never been penetrated."

"Boys and girls or just boys?" he questioned, taking me by surprise.

"I had one girl go down on me. It was a little unexpected though. It was a sleepover, and we were under the influence at the time. I had fell asleep, and when I woke up, she was down there."

He laughed.

"Did you stop her?" he inquired.

"Nope. I let her keep going, but when she was done, I told her I would cut her tongue out if she tried that shit again."

This had happened last year at Nina's sleepover. I had brought some weed brownies to the sleepover, and they were all high as fucking kites. Nina and I fell asleep on the basement couch while the other girls laid in their sleeping bags on the floor. I don't know how this girl managed to get my panties to the side without me feeling it. When I woke up, her was face was planted in my cooch. I wanted to stop her, but that shit felt so good that I just let her keep going until I was finished. She knew exactly what she was doing which told me that this wasn't her first time at the rodeo. That was my first and only experience with another girl and wouldn't happen again. I always noticed Nina checking girls out, but it never dawned on me that she was actually into women until that night. I thought maybe she just enjoyed the sight of beautiful women.

"I think you still being a virgin is a beautiful thing, Baby D. It's rare to find a flower unplucked in the hood. Make sure the person you choose to give it to will do right by you."

"Will you do right by me?"

"If I was that person, yes, but I don't think I'm that person for you. Like I said, I'm a one woman man when in a relationship, but when I'm not in a relationship, baby, I'm a dog. I bury my bones and move on. I have needs, ma, and if I'm with you, those needs can't be fulfilled unless I step out on you. I don't want to do you like that, nor do I want you to feel like I'm forcing your hand."

The entire time he spoke, I couldn't focus on anything but those beautiful pink lips and how good they would feel.

"Be careful, Chop. You might have a high school stalker on your hands. All that you just said only made me crush on you harder. So what's your real name? I know it ain't Chop."

"I can't be telling you all that. We ain't even had our first date yet, Baby D."

"This is a pre date. You picked me up, brought me food, and I told you something personal about me. It feels like a date, so spill it. What's your real name?" I asked once again.

"Only because you told me something personal about yourself. It's Kwame."

"Aww, that's a cute name."

"Thanks. What would your parents think of you hanging around a person like me?" he asked.

"You mean criminal slash bad boy?"

He laughed.

"Yeah."

"Oh, they would hate it, but I take pleasure in driving my parents crazy. I think they're expecting me to bring home a thug or maybe a girlfriend. They know me, and they know I'm way too much for one of those preppy good boys from my school. My parents are pretty cool though."

He laughed once again.

"You are a hand full, Baby D. Come on. Let's get out of here," he said, standing up and pulling my chair out for me to stand up. The way I was feeling him right now was crazy insane. He had a different kind of swag than most niggas you would see around. He was mad hood with a little bit of gentleman in him. I watched him from behind as he walked. He was pigeon toed and had this bad ass bop when he walked. He turned around and looked at me.

"Why you back there?" he asked, pulling me by the hand up to where he was and draping his arm across my shoulders. I wrapped my arm around his waist.

"I was just watching you walk."

"You were watching my butt?" he asked jokingly.

"Yep, I sure was watching that thang."

He moved my hand that was holding on to his waist down to his butt. I started laughing. I hopped on the bike behind him and placed the helmet over my head. He started up the bike and was about to pull off when a cop pulled directly in his path, blocking him from taking off.

"Cut the engine, and step off the bike," the office said from inside the car. *Ah, shit! We got caught,* I thought as I removed the helmet. I guess this was to be expected when dealing with a bad boy.

MALACHI

I had just gotten off from work and was on my way home. The sun was out, and I had the top dropped on my Audi. I felt blessed. Life didn't seem like it could get any better. Kendrick Lamar's "Humble" was on as I cruised through the streets of Passaic. I stopped at Tropical Juice Bar, got a coconut smoothie, and was heading home. My music was halted by a phone call coming into my phone. It was Maribel. I quickly answered.

"Maribel, is everything okay?" I answered, concerned. It was a little uncommon for her to be calling me. It was typically me that was calling her to speak with Mya. The last time I called for Mya, Maribel's fiancée and I got into some words. I guess he wanted to take my place as her father because he spent more time with her than I could. My father had to stop me from going to Minnesota and ripping that dude's head off.

"Everything is fine, Malachi. I'm calling to see if you could take Mya two weeks early."

"Of course, Maribel. You didn't even have to ask. Is everything okay?" I asked once again, trying to understand why she was sending her two weeks early.

"Brad wants to start our vacation early, so I figured I would see if it was okay with you if Mya came a little early."

"Sure. My mom can keep her while I work. She'll be good. Do I need to come down and get her?"

"Uh no. Our nanny is going to New York to visit some family, so you'll just have to pick her up from New York. Their flight gets in around noon, so if there's no one to pick her up from there, then Coretta is willing to bring her along with her until you get off," she explained.

"Nah, we'll be there. My parents will be able to come to get her. Send her. Don't worry about clothes. We have a bunch here for her."

"Okay, Malachi. Thank you."

I hung up the phone and continued my drive. Like I said, life didn't seem like it could get any better for me. Being able to see my daughter early was only the icing on the cake.

Once again, my music was shut down because my phone started ringing. It was an unknown number. I didn't usually answer unknown numbers, but I was in a good mood, so I answered it.

"Yo," I answered.

"Chi, I need you to come get me," Ruby's voice resonated through the phone.

"Come get you from where, Rub?"

"From Hackensack. I was picked up by the Bergen County Sheriffs."

"What the fuck you do, Ruby?" I asked, pulling over on the side of the highway.

"I didn't do anything. I was just on the back of a friend's motorcycle. They just want someone to come pick me up."

"And why didn't you call your parents?"

"Because I'm eighteen, and I don't want to die."

I laughed a little because she was right. My mother would kill her little ass if she called her. This wasn't the first time Ruby's ass had been in trouble with the police. The last time, it was because she stole the teacher's car keys and went joy riding with her car. She was thirteen when this happened. Good thing for the teacher, Ruby was taught to drive when she was eleven, so there were no damages to the car.

"I'll be there in ten minutes. Try not to get in anymore trouble before I get there, homie," I said.

"Aight."

I hung up the phone and pulled back on to the road. I got off at the next exit and went to rescue my little sis from the law.

~

I PICKED Ruby up from the Sheriff's department and dropped her back to get her car from her school parking lot. She was following behind me a few minutes ago, but she ended up turning off. I don't know where her ass was headed, but she better not end up back in jail, because big bro was gon' be busy later.

It was around 6:30 when I stepped in to the house. My mom was sitting in the living room by herself, watching TV. She must've just gotten done washing her hair because it was dripping wet.

"Hey, ma," I greeted, giving her a kiss on her cheek.

"Hey, baby. How was the rest of your day?" she asked.

"Pretty good. Yours?"

"It was okay. After I left the daycare, I took Beauty and Beast to get groomed. Then, I washed some clothes and found those in your brother's sports bag," she said, pointing to some material on the table. I walked over to the table and picked it up. It was a lace black thong.

"Sexy," I commented, causing my mom to turn around and give me a look.

"Or not."

She turned back around and started brushing her hair.

"So what, ma? Little bro getting some buns. He's a star athlete. They get all the girls. You should be proud."

"No, I shouldn't. He's only fifteen. He shouldn't be worried about sex and be worried about his school work and football."

When I didn't respond, she turned and looked at me as I looked at her like she was stupid.

"You serious right now, ma? All that boy does is worry about school and sports. He has a 3.5 grade point average and is the best running back in the state of New Jersey. He needs some kind of fun or some kind of stress outlet. Leave him alone. You worried about the wrong kid. You need to keep tabs on that menace to society daughter of yours."

"What? What she do now?" she asked.

"What hasn't Ruby done?" I responded. She shook her head.

"I'm about to send her ass to boarding school."

"You should have done that when she was two years old. I'm out. I'm about to go take a shower. I got a shorty waiting on me."

"Who? Rhyes?" she asked with a smile.

"Nah. Princess."

"Oh," she said, turning back around.

"Wait, you don't like Princess?" I asked her. When I told her about Rhyes, she was all for it, but she didn't seem to be thrilled about Princess.

"Princess is a sweet girl. She's just a little too friendly, if you know what I mean."

"She's a hoe is what you're saying?"

"I won't call her a hoe. I just saw her leave with a few different people since she's been working at the warehouse. Like I said, she's a nice girl. She's just not one I can see as a daughter in law."

"Daughter in law? Chill, ma. Aye, speaking of daughters, Mya is coming in tomorrow afternoon. You think you'll be able to pick her up from JFK tomorrow afternoon? I have to work."

"Of course I can pick my little baby up. Why didn't you tell me? I could have had her room set up for her already."

"I didn't know. Maribel called me when I was on my way home and said that Brad wanted to start their vacation early. She asked if Mya could come early."

"She know damn well she ain't have to ask. Oh my God. I need to go do some shopping," she said, jumping up from the couch.

"You don't think she has enough stuff already, Ma?" I asked. Mya still had brand new clothes from when she was a baby that she has yet to wear and won't ever get a chance to. My mother's crazy self just refuses to get rid of them. She still has clothes in the attic from when Ruby, Mega, and I were kids.

"No, she doesn't have enough. She has probably outgrown all her clothes and toys. Plus, we need some kid appropriate food for her."

"Aight, ma. Go do your thing. Now I'm about to go do mine. I'll let you know the flight information and everything when I get it."

I left out of the house and walked across the yard to the guest house. When I walked in, the lights were off, so that meant Genesis wasn't here. I sat my things down and flipped on the switch. I started walking toward the bedroom when I quickly stopped in my tracks.

"Hold the fuck up," I said as I turned back around and walked into my living room area of the house.

"What the fuck? Where the fuck is my shit?" I asked out loud after realizing that my sixty-inch screen TV was cracked, and my game system and Mac Desktop were missing. I guess she couldn't get the TV off the wall, so she just decided to smash it. I walked in the bedroom and looked for my Mac laptop. That shit was missing too. I took out my phone from my pocket and called Genesis's ass. This bitch had lost her mind. I paced back and forth as I sat there waiting for her to pick up, but the phone went straight to voicemail.

"You serious, Genesis? You took my shit? You must've forgotten that I know where ya bum ass stays. Either you have my shit back here come morning time, or I'm gon' have Ruby drag ya ass," I spat into her voicemail. I hung up the phone, went to the guest house bar, and poured a shot of Henny. I glanced at the time, realizing it was seven. I still needed to shower. My phone vibrated, and it was Princess sending me her address.

I jumped up and went to get myself ready. An hour later, I was dressed and walking out the door. The motion sensor light came on as I walked around the pool, illuminating the inside of the pool. I stopped in my tracks upon realizing what was sitting inside the pool. I walked closer. Sure enough, there was my shit sitting in the bottom of the pool.

"Oh yeah? I'm gon' have Ruby slap this bitch on sight," I said out loud as I shook my head and just said fuck it. I'd deal with this shit tomorrow.

I got inside my car and pulled out of the driveway. I enjoyed Future's new album as I followed the directions given to me by the navigation system. I was pulling up to Princess's apartment. She lived on Pomona Avenue in the Weequanic area of Newark. Her apartment building was nice. I didn't see a reason to unstrap the glock that was strapped in under the passenger seat. Whenever I came to Newark, I made sure that shit was loaded and strapped. These niggas out here were still living in that New Jersey drive life. They would try and carjack you while you were driving down a highway. They didn't give a fuck out here.

I stepped out of the car and walked into the building. I rang the doorbell to her apartment.

"Hello," her voice came through the loud speaker.

"What's up, baby? It's Malachi," I responded.

"Come on up," she said, followed by a buzzing sound. I pushed open the door and walked in. I jumped on the elevator and rode it up to her floor.

Knock! Knock! Knock!

The door immediately opened up. She stood in the doorway with a torch lighter in her hand.

"Hey, handsome," she greeted.

"Hey, baby girl. What you was in here doing with that thing?" I asked, stepping over the threshold and walking up to her. I stood at least a foot taller than her. She had to stand about five feet one at 138 pounds. Her waist was small, her hips were wide, and so was that ass. Her shape fit her height perfectly. She was a petite little thing. I could probably lift her short ass with one hand. She wore her hair wavy, and she had the front pinned up. The rest of the hair was hanging down past her shoulders. She resembled Christina Milian back in her *Love Don't Cost a Thing* days.

"I was just making the house nice for you. You know ... first impressions and all."

"I appreciate it, baby. It smells good."

"Well, that could be one of two things. Either it's the new candles I picked up from Pure Romance or the Lemon Pepper chicken and roasted garlic potatoes I cooked for you."

"Word, you cooked a nigga a meal? I wasn't expecting that. You don't look like the cooking type," I mentioned.

"I'm not. I Googled it."

"Is it too late to say I ate before I got here?"

She hit me on the arm.

"I'm joking. I can throw down in the kitchen and in the bed, baby," she said with her tongue slightly out her mouth and touching her top lip.

"I gotta see this for myself, love."

"Well then take a seat right here, and let me serve you up."

I watched as she walked over to the stove. She had on some black skinny leg jeans and a wife beater tank top tied in the back, showing off her flat stomach and the dimples in her toned back. She had on some cute pink furry slippers.

She walked over and leaned over in front of me, sitting the plate on the table. She smelled like cake batter. I wanted to lick and suck on the nape of her neck, but I would wait for later.

"This looks good, baby girl."

"Thank you. I'd like to consider myself the Master Chef."

"Let me see how this tastes first before you go doing all that talking."

I picked up the knife and fork and started digging in. I didn't stop until my plate was empty. I ate it all; chicken, potatoes, as well as the asparagus, and I didn't even eat asparagus. This fucking food was good as shit.

She was sitting across the table from me, smiling and nodding her head.

"Master Chef," she gloated.

"Aight. Aight. You got skills. Where you learn to cook like that?"

"Job corp. I studied culinary arts while there, and when I got out, I studied at Urban Arts Culinary School in Hoboken, but it was always a passion of mine. I've been cooking since I was ten years old. I got skills," she said, coming over and picking up my empty plate.

"Yes, you do. You not going to eat?" I asked her.

"No, I was picking off the food here and there as I was cooking it. This was for you."

"I appreciate it, baby girl," I said, getting up from the table and walking over to her. I cupped her face, picked her chin up, and placed a kiss on her lips. I lifted my head up, breaking the kiss. She wrapped her arm around my neck and then stood on to her tippy toes as our lips connected once again. This time, her tongue broke the barrier into my mouth as we stood there tongue wrestling with one another. I grabbed her under her ass and picked her up, wrapping her legs around my waist. She weighed damn near next to nothing.

I walked over to the couch where I sat down with her on top of me, never breaking our kiss. I tangled my fingers in her hair as I grabbed a hold of it and slightly tilted it to the side, giving me access to her beautiful neck. I started sucking on her neck, and my prediction was right. She did taste like cake batter, and her skin glistened.

"Damn, you taste good."

"Thank you. It's a new body oil I got from Pure Romance. You like it?"

"I love it. Make sure you wear this every time you come around me."

"So, there's going to be a next time?" she asked with a cute girlish smile.

"Definitely, baby. I'm feeling your vibe."

"I'm feeling you too, Malachi."

"That's good to know. So how about we slow this down a little bit, and let's get to know one another," I suggested.

"Sure thing. We can do that. You want a drink?" she asked, climbing off my lap.

"Yeah, I can go for one. What you got?"

She walked into the kitchen and reached under her countertop. She came back up with a half-gallon of Henny.

"I picked this up just for you," she said, placing the bottle on the counter top and grabbing two glasses from the cupboard. She started fixing to two Henny and Cokes. I couldn't stop watching her as she fixed the drinks. Every now and then, she would look up at me through her long lashes and smile. It really didn't make sense how fine that girl was. It didn't seem like she had any flaws so far.

She picked up the two glasses and came walking over to me.

"So where's that Ratdeer?" I asked about that ugly looking dog of hers.

"King is in his room, and don't call my baby a Ratdeer," she said, handing me a drink. She picked up the remote and pointed it toward the TV. The Pandora logo flashed on the TV and Chris Brown's Privacy started playing not too loud. She sat down on the couch next to me.

"Cheers," she said, holding out her glass, and I tapped my glass against hers.

"Cheers," I responded, taking a sip as she did the same.

"Whoa! Damn! I am not about this life."

I laughed.

"Yeah, that Hen-dog will put some hair on your chest. Are you even old enough to be drinking?" I asked.

"Yes, just about."

"Just about?"

"Yeah, I just turned twenty-one two weeks ago."

"Well happy belated, baby. How did you celebrate?"

"I didn't. I was working the warehouse. It was my choice. I'm about my coins. You feel me?"

"I definitely feel you. Where did you grow up?"

I was interested in getting to know her more. I was really feeling Princess and all of the things she'd done for me tonight. Not to mention, she was probably one of the best kissers I had ever encountered.

"I was born in East Orange where I stayed for about seven years. Then I was placed in foster care because my mom had become an addict. I was placed in two foster homes. I was molested in the first and neglected in the second one. Once I figured I'd had enough, I ran away from foster care when I was fourteen, and I started working the streets of Essex County. I figured that if I was going to be taken advantage of, I might as well get paid for it. After two years of turning tricks, I decided this wasn't the life I wanted for myself. That's when I enrolled myself into Job Corp. I got my shit together, and here I am."

I sat there stunned at her story. I honestly would have never guess she's been through so much.

"Damn, I'm sorry all that happened to you, but I'm super impressed at how you turned out after going through everything that you've been through. Thanks for sharing your story with me."

"You're welcome. I hope you don't look at me differently because of it. Whenever I like someone that's not a street nigga and I come clean about my past, they run the other way. I get what I did was dangerous and horrible. I was in survival mode back then, but I was always safe. Every six months, I'm sitting in Dr. Carson's office getting my checkups."

"I'm not here to judge you, baby girl. I'm here to get to know you. Your past doesn't even matter to me, because I wasn't a part of that. I'm here now, and that's all that matters is now."

She smiled and cupped my face with her hand.

"You're charming. You must get that from your dad because your mom seems a little uptight and judgmental."

"My mom isn't judgmental. She's just suspicious of everyone. She knows she has no right to be judgmental, because her past and present isn't squeaky clean. She has a pretty good eye for things that don't seem right. Most of the time, she's right though. My mom is pretty cool, outside of business."

"Your mom scares me, like dead ass."

She laughed and took a sip from her glass.

"Speaking of my mom, are you messing with anybody now? She said she saw you leaving with different people from the warehouse," I mentioned.

"Your mom sees everything. She probably has seen me leave with different people, but that's not because I'm sleeping with any of them. I don't have a car, so whenever I can't get a Lyft, I get rides from different people. I don't want to keep asking the same person for a ride and burn my bridges. I've only messed with one of the guys from the warehouse, and that's Jody. That was the past. We're just co-workers now. I'm not messing with anyone right now, but I want to be."

I nodded my head and then took a sip from my glass, sitting it on the table.

"Oh yeah? Who is that?" I asked.

"The Prince," she flirted with a smile as she sat across from me on her feet. I grabbed her by her waist and easily picked her up, placing her on my lap. I started untying the knot she had in the back of her shirt, running my hands up her toned back, and unhooking her bra with one hand.

"I think I like your definition of taking it slow."

Her wife beater tank had a cut in it already at the top just above her breast. I grabbed it from the top and ripped it open easily. I slid the shirt down her arms and let it fall to the floor, followed by the bra. I sat there, staring at her perfect C-cup titties.

"Is there anything about you that isn't beautiful?" I asked her.

"I have a corn on my baby toe," she answered, making me laugh.

"I'm sure that shit is beautiful too, baby."

I reached up and kissed her on the lips as I ran my hand across her nipples, catching them between my fingers and gently twisting them. I broke from the kiss and placed her nipple in my mouth. I worked my tongue over it. She had her arms wrapped around my neck as she held on to my head. I released her nipple and move on to the next, working that one over like I did the first one. A low moan escaped from her mouth, and she started gyrating on my lap. I secured her legs around my waist as I inched off the couch. I got down on the floor where I laid her on her back. I reached down, and our lips connected. We kissed passionately. DJ Khaled's "I'm On One" song was on, and the mellow beat set the mood perfectly.

All I care about is money and the city that I'm from
I'ma sip until I feel it, I'ma smoke it 'til it's done

And I don't really give a fuck, and my excuse is that I'm young
And I'm only getting older so somebody should've told you
I'm on one
Yeah, fuck it, I'm on one
Yeah, I said I'm on one
Fuck it, I'm on one

I broke the kiss as I started kissing from her cheek down her neck until I was tracing her belly button with my tongue. I bit down on the lower part of her stomach below her belly button. I looked up at her, and she was looking down at me. I sat up on my knees, and unbuttoned and unzipped her jeans. She had a tattoo of a rose and her name on the right side of her pelvis. I continued by pulling her jeans down as she lifted herself up a little so that I could get them over her plumped ass. She had on some sexy ass see-through baby blue panties where I was able to see her cleanly shaved pussy. My mouth started watering for a taste of her, but we weren't there just yet. Her thighs were thick and toned like the rest of her body.

I finally got the jeans down and from around her ankles. I peeked at her beautiful feet and noticed the corn on her baby toe that she had mentioned and laughed.

"This the corn you were talking about?" I asked.

"Yep. Ugly, right?"

"The cutest corn I have ever seen," I responded and then kissed the corn. I kissed from her feet up her thighs until I was just below her pussy. The smell that came from between her thighs were that of rose water and cupcakes. I didn't typically do this, but as an Aries, I was a risk taker. I moved her panties to the side and stuck my tongue right between her pussy lips.

"Shit," I cursed as the taste of her lingered on my tongue. Once again, I went in for another taste, this time, never stopping. She grabbed on to the back of my head as she released moan after moan, pushing my face further inside of her sweetie spot.

"Mmm, Malachi," she moaned as I continued to nibble on her. She moved her pelvis back and forth across my tongue. I sat up and removed her panties. Princess was now fumbling with my belt until she successfully got it open as well as the button and had her hands down my pants. She pulled out my dick and balls at the same time. I guess she still had skills from the past. She sat up, and in one swift motion, had my dick in her mouth. I didn't need to do anything but hold on for the ride. I don't think I'd ever had head like this. She had my dick and balls in her little mouth. It was like some kind of disappearing act she had going on. If she sucked any harder, she would be sucking the skin off me.

"Shit, Princess. You got skills, baby," I complimented as I grabbed the side of her face and started guiding myself in and out. I felt myself about to nut. She must've felt it too because she started massaging my balls which only expedited my nut.

"I'm about to nut, baby."

She didn't answer. She just nodded her head and kept on going. I guess that was my invitation to let it go, and that's what I did. I let my little mess flow right down her throat. When I was done, she sat back and watched me recuperate.

"You good, Prince?" she asked with a smile.

"Yeah, I'm good. Lay yo' ass down," I demanded as I pulled my jeans and briefs further down and pulled off my shirt. Although I had just busted a nut, I was still hard as rock. I reached in my pocket and pulled a condom. I ripped it open and rolled it down my shaft. I grabbed her by her ankles, laying her down on her back as I climbed between her legs. She gripped my dick and guided it to her opening. I pushed my way inside of her tight walls. I knew niggas were paying top dollar for a piece of this pussy.

"Why ya pussy so damn good, Princess?"

I asked a rhetorical question. Her moans resonated over the sound of the music, intensifying the moment.

"Harder," she requested, and I delivered. She pushed at my chested and then sat up, turning around on all fours.

"Damn," I spoke as I stood there appreciating the scene in front of me. I took no time diving back into that beautiful pussy of hers. I delivered every inch of this dick, and she took it like a champ, throwing her ass back at my every thrust. We were fucking like two wild street dogs in heat. I grabbed onto her waist which gave me the grip I needed to fuck it up.

The sound of smacking and moaning was loud throughout the room as we both sat there on the floor, fucking each other's brains out for two hours straight.

By the time we were finished, she laid bent over the coffee table, catching her breath. I sat on her couch in nothing but my socks and sweat, trying to catch my breath. I couldn't get enough of her sex. She was perfect.

She finally slid off the table and on to the floor.

"You fucked me up, baby," she stated as she leaned back against the couch. She picked up the glass of Henny and Coke and threw it back, making a funny face after feeling the burn from the drink. I did the same to my glass which was a mistake because my dick started to harden again. She looked over at it and then up at me smiling. Next thing I knew, she was hopping on to my lap.

"Round five?" she asked.

"I'm game."

She reached inside one of the drawers on the coffee table and pulled out a condom. She ripped it open and slid it down before she was sliding down my dick herself.

∽

AN HOUR LATER, we were walking out of her apartment building, hand in hand. I was feeling Princess, no doubt about it, but I was also feeling Rhyes. My date with Rhyes could either help my situation or just make it harder for me.

"You didn't have to walk me out, baby girl."

"I wanted to make sure you got to your car safely," she responded.

"You didn't have to do that. I'm a big boy," I said as we crossed the street to my car. When we got close, I almost swallowed my tongue.

"What the hell?" I asked out loud as I looked at the windshield of my car that was covered in something.

"What the hell is all this?" Princess asked as she touched windshield and then sniffed her finger.

"Well that's peanut butter. I think that might be jelly, and if I'm not mistaken, that clumped of brown stuff is shit."

"What childish ass person would smear peanut butter, jelly, and shit on my car?" I asked out loud.

"This looks like the work of a woman. Whose heart did you break recently?" Princess asked nonchalantly as she leaned against the car with her arms folded.

This had to be Genesis's ass, but how did she know where I was, I thought to myself.

"She could have followed you from your home and waited until you came inside. I'll go get something so that we can clean this up," Princess said as she walked across the street and into the building.

I pulled out my phone and called Genesis's number. She answered.

"You serious, Genesis?" I asked.

"I don't know what you're talking about, Malachi," she said. I could hear the laughter in her voice. I had never known her to be so fucking childish.

"Bitch, you know what the hell I'm talking about. You fucked up the shit in my house, and now you fucked up my car. Did you really take a shit on my car?"

"No, I'm a lady. I poop. I don't shit."

"Nasty bitch. I promise you—"

"You promise me what? That you're going to get your sister to drag me. Bring it on, nigga, but don't cry when your little sister gets shipped back to you in a body bag."

"Fuck you," I said, hanging up the phone just as Princess came walking over to me.

"Was that the culprit?" she asked as she handed me a pair of plastic gloves, and she put some on as well.

"Yeah, that was that bitch. I can't believe she would do something like this. I never took her as the trifling type to do some foul shit like this."

"A woman can surprise you once you break her heart. What happened between the two of you?" Princess asked.

"Nothing really. I just found out she was more into my father than she was me. I saved her by breaking it off with her because my mother started picking up on her flirtation with my father. My mom don't play when it comes to my pops."

"What? She was into your father? Your dad must be one hell of a man to make any woman overlook you."

"He aight," I answered.

"I doubt it. You seem like a great man, and he raised you, so you gotta give him some props."

She started spraying down the windshield with some Windex and Lysol, and we both proceeded to clean all the shit off my car, literally.

After an hour, we were finishing up. It wasn't perfect, but it would do until I could get it to the car wash tomorrow. I was going to make sure I paid this bitch a visit tomorrow. Princess came walking to me, removing her gloves and placing them in the bag with the shit that came off my car. I did the same.

She wrapped her arms around my waist, and I pulled her into my chest with one arm.

"Thanks, baby," I said, kissing her on the forehead.

"Anytime. Get home safe, alright?"

"Will do. I'll hit you tomorrow."

She made a puppy dog face.

"That seems so far away."

I smiled and then reached down and kissed her. I understood what she meant. I couldn't wait to see her again, myself. She had me like *Rhyes who* after one night with her.

KAYLEE

*L*ast night, I had stayed over at Enzo's and didn't feel the need to sneak out early in the morning. I was free to be with the man that I truly loved. By now, Jean Claude should have been on his way back to Paris. I never wanted to see him again.

"You ready, baby?" Enzo asked, coming into the kitchen. I was washing the dishes we had just used for breakfast. It had been a long time since I cooked a meal. We were always so busy that no one really had time to cook. We just ate out most of the time.

"Yes," I responded, drying my hands off on a hand towel. He already had my purse in his hand. I walked up to him, took it, kissed him on the lips. He was taking me to the hotel to retrieve my things that Jean left there. I never told Enzo what happened yesterday in my bedroom with Jean. Enzo had a terrible temper. He beat a guy damn near to death one time when we were on a date because the guy tried to talk to me. He was younger then. Maybe as he got older, his temper calmed.

We pulled up to the Park Ridge Marriot and looked up at the balcony to our hotel room. He put the car in park and turned it off.

"I'll be right back, okay?" I said, reaching over and kissing him on the lips.

"You sure you don't want me to come up there with you?"

"Yeah, I only have one suitcase. It shouldn't take long. If I take too long, it's room 602."

"Okay."

I dug around in my pocketbook for my room key. Once I found it, I jumped out of the car and walked into the hotel room. I waved at the concierge who seemed to be there all the damn time. I jumped on the elevator and rode it up to the sixth floor. My palms were sweating, and I was praying that Jean Claude was truly gone. *Maybe I should have had Enzo come up with me.* The elevator dinged, and the doors slid open. I slowly walked off and went down the hallway to the room. I used my key and opened the door. Upon entering the room, it appeared to be empty.

"Jean, are you still here?" I called into the room before shutting the door, just in case I needed to run back out. I checked inside the bathroom, and that too was empty. I noticed my bag sitting in the middle of the room. I let the door shut and walked inside the room. I sat the back down and unzipped it to see what all was inside and what was missing. Everything seemed to be here except for my nine thousand-dollar Cartier watch that Jean Claude bought me for my birthday.

"God damn Indian giver," I said as I zipped my bag back up.

"Looking for this?" I heard from behind me. I stood up and turned around. He was standing near the open closet door, holding up my watch.

"I thought you were gone," I said.

"You thought wrong, fiancé. I'm still here."

He shut the closet door and started walking closer to me as I backed up.

"How did you know I was here?"

"I had my little friend downstairs at the front desk give me call when you walked in the lobby. You ready to come home, baby? Our flight leaves in two hours."

He continued to walk closer to me, backing me into the wall. I had nowhere to run. I guess I was going to have fight my way out of here.

"I'm not going anywhere with you. I'm staying here where I belong."

"You mean here with that nigger?"

"He's not a nigger. His name is Enzo, if you must know, and he's downstairs waiting for me."

That's when I remembered that Enzo was sitting directly below the balcony.

"Fuck him," he said, grabbing me by the throat. I started fighting him, trying to get out his grip. With his free hand, he was attempting to shove it down the front of my jeans. I started fighting harder. I'd be damned if he was about to rape me twice, back to back.

Even with all the fight, he still managed to get his hand down my pants where he gripped my vagina and squeezed. I screamed out in pain.

"When are you going to learn that this belongs to me?"

I reached for his eyes, trying to claw at them, but he kept moving out the way, so I kneed him in the penis. He let me go, and I fell to the ground, trying to catch my breath. He went and sat on the bed, holding his penis, and I seized the opportunity to get up and run to the balcony and get Enzo's attention.

I slid the door open and ran out on to the balcony. I was about to call Enzo's name when my hair was pulled from behind. He was trying to pull me back into the room, but I wasn't letting that happen. I grabbed on to the banister and held on for dear life.

"ENZO!" I screamed.

"You screaming for him, huh? You want to be down there with him? Fine," he said, bending down and picking my legs up. I screamed as I was angled head first over the banister.

"Please, Jean, don't," I begged, hoping he would put me down.

"It's too late. You choose him over me," he spat. I held on to the banister for my life. I looked down at Enzo's car and prayed that he would look up.

Because I was hanging upside down, the blood was rushing toward my head, and I couldn't really scream for his attention. Next thing I knew, I was going over. My life flashed before my eyes. I could have sworn I was falling to my death, but when I looked up I was still holding on to the banister as my feet dangled in midair.

"HELP!" I screamed and continued to scream. I looked down and noticed Enzo's head poke out from the car.

"HELP!" I screamed again, and he disappeared into the hotel. I looked up, and Jean Claude was no longer standing there. I don't know where he had gone, but I hoped he ran into Enzo and Enzo fucked him up, quickly. I felt my hands starting to slide. I just knew I was about to die. I was six stories up, and I knew it would be a while before Enzo got here to help me. I closed my eyes and continued to pray.

I felt like I was hanging here forever before I felt someone grab my wrist. I looked up, and it was Enzo. He was pulling me up and over the banister. Once I was on safe and solid ground, I hugged Enzo and broke down crying in his arms.

"It's okay, baby. You're safe," Enzo said as he stroked my hair. No matter how much he was trying to console me, I just continued to cry. I could've been dead. *How did I not see what kind of monster Jean Claude was?* He hid it so well for so long until I felt like it was too late for me to get out.

"I'm sorry, Kaylee. I should have been up here with you. I'm going to make him pay for this. I swear," Enzo promised as he held me tight and rocked me.

ENZO

*A*fter about twenty minutes, I was able to get Kaylee calm enough to get her to the car. She sat there on the floor of the hotel room, shaking uncontrollably. *Can you blame her?* One wrong move and she could have fallen to her death. I couldn't believe he would actually throw her over the balcony the way he did. That nigga was a coward, and I was gon' make that nigga pay for this stunt he had just pulled, even if I had to fly out to Paris after that nigga.

"Sir, is there anything we can do? Maybe we could call an ambulance or the cops?" the hotel manager asked.

"Nah, I got her. She's good," I said, never making eye contact. If we got the authorities involved, then I wouldn't get the opportunity to get my hands on the pussy nigga.

"Come on, Kay. Can you stand?" I asked her. She didn't answer. She was visibly shaken up. I stood up and helped her to her feet. I wasn't about to make her walk, so I scooped her up in my arms and walked her out the room and out the hotel. When I got her to the car, I laid her in the backseat. I jumped in the car and pulled off. I was driving about ten miles over the speed limit because I wanted to run up on that nigga before he hopped on the plane.

I heard my phone vibrating on the passenger seat. I picked it up to see who was calling, rolled my eyes, and put the shit back down on the seat. It was Genesis.

Since Malachi kicked her ass to curb, she was blowing my fucking phone up. I didn't know why. What she and I had was before her and Malachi. We hooked up a few times before, and then I cut her off. A week later, she started kicking it with Malachi. I never told Malachi about me and Genesis, because that shit meant nothing to me. She was just a fuck. Like I said, I didn't know why the bitch was hitting me up.

"Kay, baby, do you want to go to my house or your parents?" I questioned. I knew I wasn't going to be staying home, so it would probably be best if I took her to her parents so that she wouldn't be alone.

"Take me to your place. I want to be with you," she muttered.

"Kay as much as I would like to be with you at this moment, I need to go handle something, so I think you should go back to your parents' until I get back. Is that okay?"

I heard her shift in the back seat to sit up.

"Where are you going?" she questioned. I hesitated before I answered her.

"I'm going to the airport."

"What? Why are you going to the airport?"

"I'm gon' catch him before he gets his ass on that plane. He ain't making it back to Paris in one piece. That's over my dead body."

"No, Enzo. You can't go there. He's a very dangerous man. You see how he was quick to toss me over a balcony. Who knows what he's bound to do to a stranger. Enzo, you can't go there."

"Kaylee, just lay back and chill."

I was getting annoyed with her talking to me like I was a pussy nigga. I never ran from a fight. That nigga may have been crazy, but he had nothing on me, especially when it came to Kaylee. I would kill someone over her, including him.

"Enzo!"

"Kaylee, I said sit the fuck back and chill!" I yelled. I had never raised my voice at Kaylee. I had never even come close to it, but I wasn't trying to hear the shit she was talking about. The rest of the ride, the car was silent. The only sound was my vibrating phone. I couldn't wait to get Kaylee out the car so that I could curse this bitch, Genesis, the fuck out. I hated when people called me back to back. If I didn't answer the first time, it meant I was busy, or I didn't want to talk to you.

Every now and then, I looked in the rearview mirror at her. She just sat there quietly, staring out the window. I decided not to say anything else to her. I would apologize later for yelling at her.

I pulled up to her parents' house and turned the car off. I was about to get out the car to go open the door for her when I heard the car door shut. I looked in the back seat, and she was already out the car and walking up the walk way to the entrance. I quickly jumped out the car to go catch her.

"Kayl—" I started to call but was met with sound of the front door slamming. I shook my head and walked back to the car. I pulled off and headed to the airport. I knew the quickest way for me to get to Newark airport was if I took the Garden State Parkway, so that's what I did.

It took me forty minutes to get there. I prayed that nigga was still here. I walked inside the airport and up to the front desk.

"Excuse me. Can you tell me when the next flight to Paris leaves?" I asked the woman. She started fumbling with her computer for what felt like forever.

"The next flight to Paris leaves in an hour," she answered.

"When did the last flight depart?" I inquired. Once again, she looked through her computer for about five minutes.

"Ahh, about four hours ago, sir. Do you need to purchase a ticket?"

"Nah. Thank you. I walked away from the desk and looked up at the screen to see which gate the flight was leaving from. When I found it, I followed the signs toward the gate. It took forever to get through this fucking airport. That was one of the reasons I hated bringing my ass here.

Ten minutes had passed by the time I made it to the gate. I searched the waiting area where all the fliers sat waiting on the flight.

I never knew how many people traveled to Paris. There were so many people waiting in this area.

I slowly walked through the crowd, trying to make out his face. I never really got a good look at him, but I would recognize his face once I saw him. It didn't take too long, because he recognized me before I did him. He got up and started fast walking in the opposite direction. I started to follow him as he bobbed and weaved through the crowd of people. I guess he thought that was going to cause me to lose him, but I was focused. I had that nigga in sight like a lion hunting a fucking zebra or some shit. The dumb ass decided to make a dodge for the bathroom like I didn't see his ass. That was his fucking mistake. He would have been better off staying mixed in with the crowd.

I walked into the bathroom where there was few people at the sink. Some were standing at urinals, but none of them were him. I looked under the two stalls, and they both appeared empty, but in the handicap accessible bathroom, there was a casting shadow coming from above the toilet. I shook my head and stood straight up, kicking the fucking door open. He was kneeling on top of the toilet seat, shaking like a little bitch. I walked into the bathroom, shutting the door behind me.

"Please just let me go back to Paris. Kaylee won't have to worry about me anymore. I swear," he begged with his hands up. I looked at him like he was stupid.

"You fucking serious right now?" I asked, walking up to him throwing a right jab so hard that the shit should have broken his face. His head went smacking into the side of the metal divider that separated this stall from the next. He stumbled off the toilet seat.

"Did you care when she begged you not to throw her off the fucking balcony?" I asked as I grabbed him by his tie and swung him into the wall on the opposite side of the bathroom. I walked up to him and started delivering blow after blow to his ribs. I'd been training with Swift in boxing since I was twelve years old, so I knew I was doing damage. Swift had me into boxing when he realized that I had anger issues after I beat a school yard full of kids. That day, I ain't care who I hit; boys, girls, or teachers. Everybody that got in my way got hit. I was expelled from that school and had to transfer somewhere else.

He had managed to slide down the wall, and I kneed the nigga straight in the face as hard as I could. That blow knocked him out cold, but that didn't stop my attack. I let him fall to the floor and continued to stomp the shit out of him as he laid there. I completely forgot that there was a bathroom full of people until someone started banging on the door.

"It's occupied," I yelled as I continued to stomp this nigga's brains out.

"Sir, this is airport police. Open the door now," that person stated, bringing me back to reality. I stopped my assault and backed up from the body that laid damn near dead on the floor in front of me. I had beat this nigga bad. I reached over and unlocked the bathroom door. There stood an officer with his hand on his weapon.

"Sir, step out of the stall," he demanded. I slowly walked out of the bathroom where they placed cuffs on me. One of the officers walked into the bathroom and checked his pulse.

"He's alive. Call for airport medical."

Shit, I was hoping I had killed that nigga, I thought to myself as they started escorting me out the bathroom.

Mega

"Mmm, I'm going to be late for class, Cassandra," I said as I pounded into her from the back. She was bent over the desk, ass in the air, and I was loving every moment of it. I pulled my penis out and bent down to lick her vagina from behind. I smacked her round butt and then inserted myself back inside of her.

"You'll be okay, Mega. I promise," she said as she threw her butt back against my pelvis.

"You feel so good, Cassie. I'm about to cum," I moaned as I felt the buildup in my balls.

"Come on, baby. Let's come together," she said as she slowed her pace down and was now doing some kind of swivel motion that I had never experienced before. That was one thing I loved about being with an experienced person. She was always showing me something new.

"I'm coming," I warned as I grabbed her by her small waist and pounded harder inside of her until I was busting inside the condom. I pulled out and backed up against the wall, trying to catch my breath. She stood up from the desk and started fixing her clothes. She removed her pink lace panties that were hooked on the heel of her high heels and walked over to me. She stuffed the panties inside my pocket.

"Add this to your collection," she ordered. I smiled and shook my head. I reached on the desk for a piece of tissue to wipe myself off. When I was done I tucked my penis back inside my pants. I picked up my book bag.

"See you after football practice, Cassandra."

I was about to walk out the door until she cleared her throat.

"Excuse me, Mr. Jones. Aren't you going to help me clean up this mess?" she asked.

"Sure thing, Principal Skylar," I said as I walked over and started helping her pick up the things we had knocked off her desk at the start of the wild sex session. This was like an everyday thing with her and I. We started having sex about five months ago. Before then, she would flirt with me occasionally. I never really picked up on it. It was my teammates who put me on to it. My focus was on football, not vagina. I had been with girls my age before, but never a woman. She approached me in the locker room after one of my games and told me she needed to speak with me back in her office.

At first, I was scared because I thought she found out about me letting Nicki give me head in the boy's bathroom, but when we got to her office, it was her who was dropping down to her knees. She pulled my gym shorts down and just did it. I didn't stop her. What guy would. Principal Skylar was so freaking beautiful and sexy. Every boy in this school had a thing for her. I looked at her every now and then, but I would have never expected to be the one having sex with her. I was the luckiest kid walking these halls.

Smack!

"What up, nugget head?" Ruby asked, smacking me in the back of the head from behind.

"The hell you want?" I asked her. I loved my sister to death and would kill for her, but she got on my last nerve sometimes. According to my mother, Ruby had been terrorizing me since she was three and I was newborn, and that has yet to change. We fought all the time, but it was all out of love. She was the reason why I was as tough as I was today. Fighting her was like fighting a nigga from the hood.

"What the hell you do? Why you coming out that skank's office?"

"She's not a skank, and she just wanted to talk to me about some colleges," I answered.

"Yeah, whatever. Look, I have something to do after school, so if Mom and Dad ask for me, tell them I volunteered to do the graduation prep."

"No, how about you call them and tell them yourself."

"I can't. You know mommy always know when I'm lying," she responded.

"And what make you think she won't figure out that I'm lying?"

"Because you won't be. You only telling her what I told you to tell her. Come on. I got you next time."

"I'll think about it," I said, putting in the combination, removing my notebook, shutting my locker, and attempting to walk away from Ruby, but I ended up walking right into her. She had on a sad puppy dog face, and her hands were clasped together.

"Fine. Now will you move? I need to get to class."

"Why you even going? It's the end of the school year. They stopped taking attendance a week ago."

"Because I want to. Now get the hell out of my way."

"Thank you, baby bro. I love you," she said, kissing me on the side of my neck. I mushed her ass straight in the forehead. I don't know what the hell her ass was about to get into, but knowing Ruby's ass, I don't think I wanted to know so that I wouldn't be forced to rat on her.

PRYCE

J woke up to kisses being placed on the back of my thighs as I laid naked on the bed in nothing but the sheets to the hotel room wrapped across my upper body.

"Mmm, that feels good," I said as I laid there and enjoyed the feeling of his lips kissing up my legs. He removed the blanket that covered my bare butt. He bit down on my left butt cheek and then the right. He dragged his tongue up my spine until he got to my neck. He was now lying on top of me with his mouth pressed against my ear.

"What you wanna do today?" he asked, whispering in my ear as he wiggled his way between my legs.

"Well, I was thinking we could visit the Mus—" I said and was interrupted by the pain of him entering me. Although we'd had sex plenty of times since being down here, I still felt pain.

"Museum of Natural Science," I continued.

"We can go wherever your big heart desires," he said as he pushed in and out of me. My body had tensed up as he rode my body like his own personal pony.

"You know it'll feel much better once you loosen up and stop being so tense."

I gripped the sheets as I tried to loosen up like Kevin suggested. He turned me around as he entered me once again, this time from the front. He placed his face in the crock of my neck and started sucking on my neck so hard that I didn't feel pleasure. It was all pain.

"Ease up just a little, baby," I requested, pulling away just a little.

"Oh, sorry, sweet girl. I just be getting so carried away. You just so beautiful and tender," he said as he went down to my B-cup breast and sucked one inside of his mouth. I grabbed on to his bald head, and I enjoyed the feeling of his tongue flicking across my nipple. That was until he bit down on my nipple. At times, he could be so gentle with me, and other times, he could get a little rough.

When we first arrived at the hotel, he wasted no time throwing me on the bed and making love to me. Not that I minded, but I just wanted to get settled in first and take a shower. He had other plans in mind. The first day here, we ended up staying in the entire night and having sex as well as the second day. Today, I was determined to get out of this hotel and enjoy the city of Houston and all that it had to offer. I couldn't stay two more weeks stuck up in this hotel room.

"Ou, that's hurts," I complained as I tried to release my breast from his mouth.

"Is there anything I do that doesn't hurt?" he asked, pulling out of me and standing up from the bed.

"Yes, but we been in this hotel having sex for the last two days. My body is a little sore. I'm still new at this. We need to slow it down just a little. Give my body a little break."

"Yeah, okay. How about I go run us a bath and we wash each other before we spend the entire day in the scolding Houston heat?"

"That's sounds like fun. I'll see you in there," I said. I stood up off the bed and walked to the mirror. I brushed my hair into a messy bun on the top of my head.

"Seriously?" I asked out loud as I noticed a huge mark on my neck. That must've happened when Kevin was sucking on my neck. Was he back in high school? This looked so horrible. I searched my suitcase for my concealer and applied it to the ugly hickey on my neck.

Once I had it covered completely, I put on a T-shirt, grabbed my phone, and went out on to the balcony and FaceTime my dad. It rang a few times before he picked up. He looked like he was at the gym.

"Hey, baby girl," he greeted.

"Hey, daddy."

"How's it going out there in the Motherland?" he asked.

"It's fine and really, really hot. Another week of this, and I'll be ready to come home. What you up too?" I asked, trying to throw him off from his questioning.

"At the gym with Uncle Swift."

"Hey, niece, how's Africa?" Uncle Swift asked, popping his head in the phone camera.

"It's fine, Uncle Swift. What you doing back in the gym? Did you get cleared to start working out again?" I asked. A few years back, Uncle Swift used to fight mixed martial arts. He was partially paralyzed during a fight and only had feeling on his left side. He went through a combination of surgery and physical therapy to get better, and it helped. He regained all movements, but was told he couldn't participate in any strenuous activity which included fighting and gym workouts.

"Who's the adult here?" he asked.

"Apparently I am. Why are you back in the gym?"

"I'm not going overboard. Chill out, niece. Stop being so worried about what's going on here in the States and enjoy your trip."

"Alright, mister. Dad, where's mom?" I asked. I looked up, and Kevin was standing there at the door, telling me to come on. I put up my hand, telling him to give me a minute.

"She rode with Camilla to pick up Mya from the airport," he answered.

"Oh my God. Mya is back? I wish I was there," I said with a sad face.

"She's staying the whole summer, so she'll be here when you get back."

"Okay. Let Mom know I called, and I'll call you guys later."

"Okay, baby girl. Be safe. Ttyl."

"Dad, please don't say that again. Love you. Talk to you later," I said, hanging up the phone. I stood up from the chair and walked back inside the room. For some reason, I suddenly started to become homesick. I was ready to go home after three days.

I removed the T-shirt and walked into the bathroom where Kevin sat inside the bathtub. I climbed in and sat between his legs as he immediately started washing my back.

"Have you spoken to your wife?" I questioned.

"Yeah, this morning before you woke up," he answered. He told his wife that he was acting as a guest preacher at a church in Atlanta for three weeks. His wife was a mean woman who felt like she could talk to anyone however she wanted, including her husband. She spoke to Kevin like he was shit under her two-inch church heel. She thought she was better than everyone in the church just because her husband was the pastor at the church. Little did she know that her daughter was the biggest hoe walking around that church, and her husband was cheating on her with a teenager.

Before Kevin and I started messing around, I used to go to their house all the time with Jo. Whenever Kevin would come home, she would make me leave. Maybe she noticed the way he looked at me the same way I noticed.

"I love you, Pryce. You know that?" he asked as he ran the sponge across my back.

"I know. I love you too, Kevin," I responded as I sat there thinking about home.

MALACHI

I rushed home after work because I was excited to see my baby. My mom picked her up earlier and then called and told me to get home as soon as I got off. After that last bell rang, I didn't even change out my gym clothes. I just grabbed my shit and jumped in the car. I was excited, but at the same time, I was concerned as to why my mother told me to get home in a hurry.

My phone rang, and it was Rhyes. I hit the ignore button and placed my phone back inside the cup holder. She had been calling and texting me all day, but besides me responding with a hello text, I was kind of ignoring her. It was nothing she did, but after the night I'd had with Princess, I was kind of set on her. Princess was dope, and I was really feeling her. That still didn't give me the right to treat Rhyes the way I was. I suddenly felt guilty. I picked up my phone and dialed Rhyes' number.

"Hello, you," she answered.

"Hey, beautiful. How are you?" I asked.

"Um, I'm fine, although I feel like I been getting the cold shoulder from you all day."

"Yeah, I'm sorry about that. My daughter came in town today, and all I been thinking about is getting home to her. I apologize. I swear."

"It's okay. I get it. How about you give me a call when you get a chance."

"I'll definitely do that. We're still on for Friday," I stated.

"Okay. See you then, and hopefully, I'll talk to you later."

"For sure."

I hung up the phone and pushed down on the gas as I drove down the Garden State Parkway to get home quicker.

~

I PULLED up to my house and jumped out. It had been almost a year since I'd seen my baby girl, and I just wanted to hold her in my arms just for a minute.

"Where my baby girl at?" I asked upon walking into the living room where my mom, Aunt Blaize, and Mya sat. I ran over to her, picked her up off my mom's lap, and gave her the tightest hug ever.

"Hey, baby. Daddy missed you," I spoke as I held her sandy brown head against my chest. She had grown so much since I last saw her.

"I got iPad," she said, showing me the white device in her hand."

"Oh yeah? Where you get that from?" I asked her. She turned and pointed at my mom.

"Grandma brought that for you?"

She nodded her head up and down. My baby girl was so beautiful. She came a long way from being born premature and having to stay in an incubator for months, to now being two years old, walking around in good health, and able to form sentences. We were told that her development would be delayed, but she was perfect.

I walked over to the couch and sat down with her on my lap.

"Oh hey, Aunty B," I said, reaching over and giving her a kiss on the cheek.

"Hey, nephew."

"So what happened? Why did you ask me to hurry straight home?" I asked, looking over at my mother.

"After we got back home, I had ran Mya a bath, and as I was removing her clothes, I noticed these," she said, standing up and walking over to us. She kneeled down in front of Mya and me and attempted raise the bottom of Mya's dress, but Mya stopped her.

"Can grandma see your leg one more time baby? Please," she begged with her hand clasped together and a sad face on. Mya thought about it and then nodded her head yes. My mom began to raise her dress again until her legs were revealed. It felt like my heart was being squeezed and it was hard for me to breathe.

"What happened to her?" I asked with concern.

"I don't know, but her entire body is covered in black and blue bruises," she answered.

"You telling me somebody been abusing my daughter?"

"It appears, but the only way we can be sure is if we take her to see a doctor and take her to get examined."

"What if they think we had something to do with this?"

"We can take her to Dr. Barnes. He knows we're good people. Besides, he owes me a favor."

"Okay," I agreed.

"Mya, baby, who did this to you?" I asked, pointing at her leg where there was black and blue bruise. She pointed at her bruise.

"Ouch," she said, causing my heart to break.

"Who did this, baby?" I asked once again.

"Brad and mommy."

"Both of them did this shit? Oh my fucking God. Come on, baby. Daddy is going to take you to see a doctor, okay?"

"Will I get oddipop?" she asked.

"Yeah, Daddy will find you a lollipop, okay?"

"Okay," she said, jumping off my lap. I wiped a tear from my eye as I stood up off the couch. I could seriously murder someone today.

"Aye," my mom said, stopping me in my tracks.

"She will not step foot in that state or that house again. We will fight tooth and nail for our little girl. I told you this before. No one fucks with my family. They will pay. I promise you."

I nodded my head, agreeing with my mother. She wiped away another tear that managed to escape my eyes. We piled into my mother's car and made our way to get my baby girl checked out.

"Ahh, keeping up with the Jones," Dr. Barnes said as we walked into his office. Dr. Barnes was our pediatrician. He treated my siblings and I as well as Trey since we were kids. He still treated Ruby and Mega. He had a gambling problem and had managed to get himself in a pretty bad situation where he was on the verge of losing his practice. It never happened, and I think my mom and pops had something to do with it. I'm guessing that's what she meant by him owing her a favor.

"Hey, Dr. Barnes," I greeted.

"Malachi, long time no see."

"Yeah, I don't have a reason to come anymore."

"I saw Trey not too long ago. I treat his son, lil' Trey."

"It's good to know he's been well taken care of. We need a favor, Dr. Barnes. I picked up my granddaughter from the airport today because she's staying the summer. When I got her home to wash her, I found bruises on her body. We believe she's being abused at home with her mom. I need you to examine her for me, off the record. We just need to know the extent of the abuse."

"Wow. You know I am required to report abuse when it comes to kids. I can lose my medical license if it gets out that I ignored it," Dr. Barnes informed.

"You won't have to worry about it getting out. I would never do anything to jeopardize your license."

He sat there for a minute.

"Okay," he answered.

"Follow me."

He led us to an examination room where he instructed me to remove Mya's clothes and put a gown on her. While I was taking off her clothes, I noticed all the bruises that my mom was talking about. They covered her back and legs. They looked as if they were made with some kind of stick or pole of something. Her beautiful tan skin was now red, blue, and black.

"Daddy cry," Mya laughed, placing her finger under my eye. I don't understand how someone would want to hurt someone so beautiful and innocent, her own mother, at that. She knew firsthand what this little girl went through when she was younger, and she still chose to cause her so much pain.

"Yeah, baby. Daddy just happy to see you. Give your daddy a big hug," my mom insisted. Mya stood up on the examination table and wrapped her arms around my neck, giving me the tightest hug ever. I wrapped my arms around her little body and returned the hug.

"Do you want to go sit outside with Blaize? I can stay in here with her," my mom asked.

"Nah, I'm good. I want to be in here with her."

The door came open, and Dr. Barnes walked in.

"Are you Princess Mya?" Dr. Barnes asked, sitting on the table next to her. She nodded her head yes and smiled at him.

"Good because I have this for Princess Mya," he said as he brought his hand from behind his back and showed her the lollipop he had for her. She took it from him and immediately started unwrapping it.

"Okay, can I take a look at your legs?" he asked her, pointing down to her legs. Once again, she pointed down to her leg and said ouch.

"Ouch, I know. Can you lie down for me, Princess Mya?"

She ignored him. I stood up from the chair I was sitting in and gave him a hand.

"Come on, baby. Can you lie down for daddy?"

"No," she answered. I looked over at Dr. Barnes.

"It's okay. I can do it another way," he said.

"Princess Mya, can you stand up for me?"

She stood up on the examination table, and Dr. Barnes picked her leg up and started moving it around. He did the same to the other one.

"No signs of any fractures. Let's check her arms."

As soon as he lifted her arm above her head and bent it behind her a little, she winced in pain.

"I'm sorry, Princess Mya."

He carefully put her arm back down against her side. He did the same to the other arm, and this one appeared to be okay. He pressed down on her belly, and everything seemed to be fine internally.

"Okay, Princess Mya, you're all done," he said, fixing her gown.

"There are two things in particular that concern me … One being her left shoulder. I would like to get an X-ray done on that shoulder. Is that okay?"

"Yeah, that's fine. What's the second thing?" I asked.

"The second thing that I am concerned about is," he started to say and he hesitated.

"Possible sexual assault."

"Oh my God. I can't do this," I said, walking out of the room to get my head together. I couldn't be in there right now. I felt like I was going to crumble into a puddle of tears and pity. While I was chilling back here living my life, my baby was somewhere being abused.

"Hey, nephew," Aunt Blaize said, coming toward me. I wiped my face and stood up. I looked up at her, and she didn't say anything. She just stood there staring at me. It was like she knew what I needed at that moment, and it wasn't words. She walked closer to me and just wrapped her arms around my neck, hugging me tightly. I wrapped my arms around her, and that's when I broke down into pieces. Tears flooded my face, and I silently cried my heart out on her shoulder. I didn't want Mya to hear me crying, so I cried silently.

"She's only two," I cried.

"And she's strong. She's a Jones. Even with her going through what she went through, she still manages to smile and make everyone around her happy. You have to stay strong for your daughter. She has a poor excuse for a mother, so go in there and be a father for her. If there's one thing I know, it's that they will pay. No one hurts this family and gets away with it. No one does. Now you wipe your face and go in there with your daughter."

She gave me one last hug and walked back to the waiting room. I went and found the restroom. When I got inside, I turned on the water and washed my face. I looked in the mirror and told myself to be strong. I had to prepare myself to walk back into the room. Being physically abused was one thing, but being sexually abused was another. She was only two.

I dried my face with a paper towel and walked back to the room.

"Hey, I'm back."

"You're okay, baby?" my mom asked.

"No, I'm not, but I'll get there. What do you need to do to determine if she was sexually abused?" I questioned.

"I would need to examine her vaginal area, but I can tell that she's not going to let me do it here by the fact that she wouldn't even lay down for me. What I can do is make a house visit once you get her down to sleep. I can do the examination, and she won't feel anything. It's just a quick examination."

"Okay, can you come by tonight?" I asked.

"Sure. I'll be there, Malachi. In the meantime, let's get the X-ray done to see what's causing her pain."

I nodded my head in agreement. He left the room, leaving me, my mom, and Mya in the room alone.

"We are going to get through this, baby," my mom said, clasping my hand. I looked down at her hand inside mine and knew that she would never tell a lie. I believed her every word, and if she said we were going to get through this, then I knew we were.

After we left Dr. Barnes office, we went back home where my dad waited for us. The first thing he did was pick Mya up and shower her with kisses as he held her tightly. He then looked over at me and grabbed me by the shoulder, pulling me in for a hug. Although I was twenty-four, he held me like he did when I was a young boy.

"She's going to be alright. You hear me?" he asked, picking my head up and looking me straight in the eyes.

"Yeah."

He let me go, and we all walked in to the living room and sat down. My father put Mya down on the floor, and she took off running. Dr. Barnes had placed a shoulder sling on her arm to keep it stabilized. She had a small shoulder fracture which Dr. Barnes said could have come from her falling hard on an outstretched arm or from her arm being yanked. She had to keep that sling on for three to four weeks. I don't know how they expected a two-year-old to keep their shoulder stabilized for so long.

"What did Dr. Barnes say?"

"Three to four weeks in the sling. Bruises seem recent, like within the last week or so. He wants to come here once she falls to sleep and check to see if she may have been sexually abused, but I'm not sure if I want to know."

"It's best that we know so that we can get her the treatment she'll need. You listen to me, son. You don't worry about them two. Let me and your mom deal with them. You focus on being a father to that little girl by providing her with the love and nurture she wasn't receiving from her mother."

"I can do that, but I can't not do anything about the two of them putting their hands on my daughter. She's only two. What could she have done so bad that would make them want to cause harm to her? I can't not do anything, dad. I have to do something. That's my baby."

"I understand, but as of now, I need you to chill. They will get what's coming to them. I put that on my kids."

My father was a very laid-back person. I don't think I'd ever seen him stressed out about anything. Even with the current situation, he still remained calm. An outsider would have thought that he didn't really care, but I knew once he swore on his kids that he cared and was going to make shit happen.

RUBY

"I can't believe you let me drive your Porsche," I squealed as we entered the Holland Tunnel, heading to Canal Street to do some shopping. I needed something to wear to my graduation and a cute bathing suit for my pool party. It was bound to be the party of the year. I invited so many people. Damn near the whole school and people from the hood were coming. My parents were going to flip, especially my dad. He didn't like strangers in his house, but the way I looked at it, they weren't going to be in the house. They were going to be in the back yard. If they needed to use the bathroom, I would just have them use Malachi's bathroom.

"Yeah, I can't either. I must really like yo' little ass. I don't ever let anybody drive my shit. Hell, I barely drive my shit."

"You like me?" I asked, blushing bright red.

"Yeah, I do."

"Good, because I like you too. So much so, I want to give you a ticket to my graduation and my graduation party. Are you going to come?" I asked him.

"If you're inviting me, then hell yeah. I'll be there for you, Baby D. I wouldn't miss it."

I was happy that he agreed to come. I knew my mom and dad

weren't going to be happy, but I didn't care. It was my day. I was eighteen which legally made me grown, so their feelings didn't matter.

I turned back and looked at the road ahead of me. I didn't want to crash his car. He would never speak to me again.

"You are handling this car pretty well, Baby D."

"I like fast things. I've been trying to take my mom's Ferrari out for a spin since forever."

"Word? Ya moms got a rari?" he asked.

"Yeah, she never drives it. She keeps it covered in the garage. I told her she should just give it to me since she's not going to use it."

"Word."

We exited the tunnel on to Canal Street. It was late in the afternoon. It was rush hour, so the traffic was insane, and I was a very impatient person. We were only in traffic for about five minutes, but to me, it felt like three hours. I was in a fast ass car, and I wanted to just go. The traffic light turned green, and I pulled off. There was this girl who decided to walk her big ass head out into the street while the light was green, so I decided to play with her a little bit. I pushed on the gas and sped into her direction, pressing on the breaks and stopping the car before it reached her. She was scared as hell.

"Hit me, bitch. I want you to. Make me some motherfucking guap today."

The girl talked shit.

"Shut the fuck up. You won't get shit but a body cast or a casket, bitch. Now keep it walking before I smack yo' ass!" I yelled back.

"You won't do a god damn thing," she responded as she kept walking like everything was all peachy. I put the car in park, unbuckled my seat belt, and hopped out the car in the middle of the busy Canal Street.

"Chill, Baby D!" Chop called with a laugh, but I ignored him and just kept walking in the direction of the girl. She must've though I was pussy because she continued to walk, never looking behind her.

"Yo, bitch!" I yelled, getting her attention. She turned around and was greeted with smack to the right side of her cheek. She stood there stunned at what I had just done. I turned around and walked back to the car, calm and cool. Cars were blowing their horns because I was blocking traffic, but I didn't give a fuck. That bitch was about to put some respect on my name, even if she didn't know my name. I got back in the car, put my seatbelt on, and put the car back in drive.

"You's a wild girl, Baby D."

"Trust me. You haven't seen anything yet."

"Oh really? Well I can't wait to see what more you have to offer."

BRYCE

I was sitting in front of my laptop, getting some beats ready for the teen party I was supposed to be DJing at Friday. I had some new and old school blends that I was going to be spinning. I liked spinning for the teens way better because they knew how to have more fun than the adults. I could play anything, and the kids would still dance. I played some Kodak Black and Designer for the older crowd. They started calling for someone named the Sandman to remove me from the stage until I played some Montell Jordan and 112. Then they all started vibing.

My phone started buzzing next to me, alerting me to a text message. I opened it up, and it was from Marco. I picked up the phone and sat back in the chair, reading his message.

Marco: I have some things for you to try on. You wanna slide through.

Not only was Marco somebody I was messing around with. He was also a stylist. Whenever I was spinning at a club or whenever Nico and I were performing, Marco would track down the flyest gear for us to rock that night. Marco was well-known for his styling skills.

Me: Do I really need to come try them on? You know my size

and my style. Just send me a picture of them. I'm working right now.

I knew this was just his way of getting me to come over to his house. I told him the other day when I was over there that I wanted to slow things down. Of course, he overreacted. He had this whole little hissy fit. Marco was something else sometimes. He really was supposed to be a female because he had the emotion of one.

Marco: Well every fabric has a different stretch and fit, so yes, you really do need to come try it on Bryce.

Me: Aight, be there in a few.

I laughed and sat my phone back on the desk. I finished up what I was doing and went to take a quick shower. I threw on some grey Nike sweats and a white T-shirt. I put on my platinum crucifix, sprayed some Victoria Secret's Very Sexy for men cologne, grabbed my keys and cellphone, and left out the room.

I was walking down the hallway, about to hit the stairs, when I heard what sounded like crying. I looked inside my parents' bedroom, and it was empty. KJ and Pryce weren't here, so it had to be coming from Kaylee's room. I knocked on her door and waited for her to tell me to enter, but she never did.

"Kaylee," I called. It took her a while before she answered. I wasn't expecting her to be here. I thought she was staying at the hotel with her fiancé who seemed to never be around.

"Yeah," she answered.

"Are you okay?"

I waited for her to answer, but she didn't, so I took it upon myself to walk inside her bedroom and shut the door behind me. When I got in, she was lying in the bed under the covers.

"Kay, are you okay?" I asked her as I walked around to the other side of the bed. She had tears dripping from her eyes down her nose and on to her pillow. She dapped her beautiful face with a piece of tissue.

"No, but I'll be okay," she said, sitting up in her bed and displaying a forced smile.

"Do you want to talk about it?"

"Thanks, Bry. I do, but not right now. I'm just going through something that I need to understand myself, but once I do, I'll talk to someone."

"Okay. Remember what you told me about my little secret? That goes both ways. You can always talk to me. I may be a teenager, but I understand a lot. Your secrets are safe with me."

"I know. Thanks, little brother," she said, reaching over and giving me a hug.

"Where you on your way to, smelling all grown and sexy?"

I laughed.

"I have a stylist who has some outfits for me to try on for the party Friday, so I'm going over there real quick."

"Alright. Be safe, little brother. Love you."

"Love you too, Kay."

I stood up from the bed and walked out of the bedroom, shutting the door behind me. I raced out of the house, jumping into my red 2016 Toyota Scion TC. My parents had brought me and Pryce matching cars for our sixteenth birthday. I had red, and Pryce's car was an iceberg blue. They presented them to us at our Sweet Sixteen last year. Our seventeenth birthday was coming up in a month, so I was dying to see what they were going to get for us.

I missed my sister. I couldn't wait until she came back home. Besides Kaylee, Pryce was the only one who knew about me messing with Marco. Pryce was my twin but also my best friend who knew almost everything about me. We kept no secrets from each other. It was hard for us to do so because it was like we were telepathically connected. Whenever she got hurt, it was like I felt the pain she was experiencing. Whenever I got hurt, five minutes later, she was either calling me or coming into my room and asking me if I was okay. This had been going on since we were young.

I started my car and hooked up my phone to the car radio. I turn on the driving playlist and pulled out of the driveway. It took me almost thirty minutes to get to Marco's house in Teaneck. Marco wasn't from the hood. He was actually one of those privileged kids who was spoiled by their well-established parents, kind of like myself.

Marco hung out in the hood because people in his area made him feel self-conscious about himself. They would stare and laugh at him because of the way he dressed and walked. But what they couldn't see was the person he was inside. He had a big personality and an even bigger heart, but don't get on his bad side. That big heart became a big block of ice. He spazzed out on me a few times for no fucking reason. Then he would call the next day, apologizing.

I pulled out my phone and texted him that I was here before I got out of the car. I walked up to the house and around to the back to where his studio was. His studio also doubled as a bedroom. Although he had a bedroom inside the house, he chose to sleep out in the shed which was where his studio was located.

I walked into the backyard and toward the shed. Marco opened the door and then walked away. Typically, he would be greeting me at the door, but not today. I guess he took me serious when I said I needed to cool things off.

When I walked into the shed, he was standing over by a rack of clothes. He said nothing to me as he started taking some things off the rack. He handed me the clothes to try on and pointed toward the changing area he had in the corner of the room.

"So you not gon' talk to me, Marco?" I asked him.

"I literally have nothing to say to you. I'm just doing my job. Now if you don't mind going to try those clothes on because I need to know if I need to find you something else when I go to the mall," he said, rolling his eyes and turning back toward the rack of clothes. I shook my head and walked over to try on the clothes.

The first outfit was some white Balmain distressed jeans, with a Balmain red sleeveless hoodie, and some white Rip Off ankle strap sneakers. This shit looked dope. I didn't even need to try on the rest. I had my outfit right here.

"How I look?" I asked Marco. He turned around and looked me up and down.

"Fly as always. I got skills."

"Exactly. Like I said, I didn't need to come try it on. I trust ya style, love."

153

"Okay, so are you going to try the second one on or not?" he asked.

"I don't need to," I said.

"Okay, cool."

He turned around and started fixing the clothes on the racks wile I went and changed out of the clothes and back into my sweats. When I came back out, he was sitting on the bed and picking at his nails.

"Are you satisfied?" he asked.

"Yes, I am as always."

"Cool," he said with his hands out. I walked over to him and slapped him on his extended hand, knocking it down. He picked it back up.

"Excuse me. Run me my money," he said, looking up at me. I reached in my pocket and pulled out the five hundred-dollar bills.

"If you want this, you gotta stop being mad at me," I said.

"I don't have to stop doing anything. I worked for this money, now run it."

"What do I have to do to get you to be my friend again?"

"What kind of friend are we speaking of?"

"The kind of friend that speaks to me when they see me and don't give me the cold shoulder like you are doing now."

"It's hard to be that friend when every time I see you, all I can think about is you inside my mouth," he revealed. I placed my hand on his shoulder and squeezed it firmly, nothing too hard.

"Try to think of something else," I insisted as I grabbed the bag with the clothes in it off the bed. I started walking toward the door.

"Bryce, wait. Please don't go," he begged, running up to me, grabbing my hand. It confused me because just a minute ago, he was barely saying anything to me. I turned around.

"I have to. I got things to do."

"You can stay here and do me if you want."

"Nah, Marco. It won't be none of that anymore. I told you."

He grabbed on to my penis through my sweats and started stroking it. I couldn't lie. It felt good, but I knew it was wrong. I couldn't lead him on like that. I removed his hand.

"Marco, stop. Please. You deserve someone that's going to be proud to be seen with you in public, and it ain't me. What we had was great, like really great, but it can't be anymore. Can you understand that for me?" I asked.

"But I love you, Bryce," he said, wrapping his arm around my waist, then reaching up and kissing me on the lips. I didn't move. I let him kiss me. Once again, his hand was on my penis, and I didn't remove it. Marco placed his hand inside my sweatpants, grabbed a handful of my penis, and gripped it firmly. He started moving it in a jerking motion. It felt good.

I grabbed on to his face and kissed him back as he loosened my pants and pulled them down. He dropped down to his knees, pulled out my penis, and quickly shoved it in to his mouth. His strong throat consumed me whole, spit me back out, and sucked me in again.

"Shit," I said out loud as I held up my T-shirt with one hand and the back of his head with the other one, pushing myself further down his throat. I don't think I'd ever come across a girl who could give me head like this. This shit was addictive. I promised myself that this was the last time, and I meant it this time.

KAYLEE

I sat up in bed with my phone to my ear. I had been in the bed all day since Enzo dropped me off so that he could go chase down Jean Claude. I appreciated him trying to protect me and make Jean pay for what he did, but I didn't want him getting himself in trouble over it. I had been trying to call Enzo for the last four hours, and he wasn't answering his phone. I was starting to get worried.

I called once again, and again, the phone just rang before it went to voicemail. I hung up and called Malachi's number, but an operator came up, telling me the number was not in service. I jumped out of the bed to find someone I could get Malachi's number from. My brothers were gone, but I smelled something cooking and figured it was my mom cooking. I ran down the stairs to the kitchen.

"Hey, ma," I greeted her upon entering the kitchen. She turned and looked at me and smiled.

"Hey, baby. I didn't know you were still here. I though you would have been with Enzo."

"No, I can't get in touch with him. Can I use your phone to call Malachi? I don't have his new number."

"Sure, but he might not answer. He's going through something with Mya."

"Mya's here? I have to go over there and meet her."

"She's a sweet little girl."

I picked up my mom's phone and sat down at the table. I dialed Malachi, and like my mom said, he didn't answer, but that didn't stop me from trying. I called again and waited as it rang. He answered.

"Hey, Chi. It's Kay," I greeted.

"Hey, cuz. What's going on?" he asked.

"Have you heard from Enzo? I have been trying to call him for the last few hours, and he's not answering."

"Nah, when was the last time you spoke to him?"

Because I didn't want my mom to hear, I got up and ran back up the stairs to my room and shut the door.

"Something happened with Jean and I, and Enzo was around. He dropped me off home and said he was going to airport to meet with Jean. I haven't heard or spoke to him since."

"Damn, I'll check with the jail see if his ass was picked up. I'll call you back."

"Don't worry about calling back. I want to come over and see Mya, so I'll be there in a few."

"Aight."

I hung up the phone and went downstairs to give my mom her phone back. I had returned the rental to the company, so I didn't have a car anymore. The car I had before I left for Paris, I gave my mom permission to donate it. It was a piece of shit because my dad didn't trust me with a brand-new car, so he bought me a hoopty to get around. I failed my driver's test five times. I finally passed when I turned eighteen, and I think that was because the tester of Department of Motor Vehicles felt bad for my non-driving ass. I was much better now. I had a lot of practice back in Paris. Maybe I could get my parents to buy me a new car now.

I changed into some black stretch pants, a black tank top, my black and gold Royalty Jordans. I grabbed my purse and left out the room.

"Ma, can I borrow your car so I can over to see Mya?" I asked. She turned and looked at me like I had just lost my mind.

"Uhh, I can drive you, baby," she answered.

"Come on, Ma. I can drive now. You see I brought the rental back in one piece. I promise I won't mess your car up."

She was a little hesitant at first, but then she pointed to her purse. I ran over and grabbed her keys out her bag and stopped by her, kissing her on her cheek and running to the garage door. I jumped in her 2017 F-type Jag coupe. I loved this car. My dad brought it for her for her birthday. He called me when he was at the dealer and asked for my opinion about the car before he bought it.

I pulled out of the garage, dropped the top, and peeled off. I know I gave my mom a heart attack with the way I pulled off. I wouldn't be surprised if she started blowing my phone up.

Their house wasn't too far from us. It was only like ten minutes down Highway 17. They lived in Upper Saddle River which was for the super-rich, and we lived in Mahwah which was for the financially stable people, like us.

I pulled up to my family's outrageously humongous house. I was surprise I remembered how to get here. I pulled up to the long straight driveway that was lined by beautifully bloomed Japanese Cherry trees. The whole family helped plant these trees like thirteen years ago for Ruby's fifth garden birthday party. They had grown so much in the last thirteen years. Ruby probably didn't even pay attention to them. I was with my mom and Aunt Camilla when Aunt Camilla purchased all these trees. She paid one hundred dollars per tree, and there had to be about fifty trees that lined this driveway.

I pulled up to the front of the house and jumped out of the car. I locked the door, ran up to the house door, put in the keypad code and walked straight in. My aunt and uncle were sitting on the couch. They looked at me.

"Where's Chi?" I asked. Both of their heads jerked back at the same time.

"I know Paris has different rules and traditions than the US, but

I'm sure you still supposed to say hello when you walk in someone's house," Aunt Camilla stated.

"I'm sorry. Hey, family," I said, reaching down and kissing them both on the cheek.

"That's better. What you doing here? Ya mama let you drive her car?"

"Yeah, I had to beg. Maybe she'll talk my dad into buying me a car, orrr you can just let me drive the rarri," I said with a cheesy smile, knowing damn well she wasn't about to let that happen.

Uncle Troy and I started laughing at the look she was giving me. She had the Judge Judy face on.

"I was joking. Chillax."

"Malachi is upstairs with Mya."

"Thanks, Uncle Troy."

I ran up the stairs, taking two at a time until I reached the top. I walked down the long ass hallway.

"Chi!" I called.

"What's up, Kay?" he said, sticking his head out one of the bedroom doors. I walked down the hall to where he was standing. I gave him a hug before we entered the room. It was beautifully decorated.

"Aww it's really cute in here. I had this same bedroom set," I said, walking in and seeing the pearl princess canopy bed with gold details. It was exactly the same as the one I had when it was just me and my dad.

"That's because it is yours. Your father was trying to throw it away once y'all moved out of your old house, and my mom, the hoarder, wouldn't allow it. She took it and put it in storage. When Mya came to visit last year, my mom finally put it to use," Malachi explained.

"That's so cool. This must be the princess. Hey, Mya," I said, sitting down on the carpet next to her.

"I'm your cousin, Kaylee."

She looked up at me and offered me her princess doll. I started playing with her when I noticed the bruises on her leg. I lifted her dress just a little to get a better look.

"What happened? Did she fall?"

"Nah, we'll talk about it later. So, your nutcase boyfriend was arrested this morning for beating up on ol' dude. He's going to be taken in front of the judge at seven. I got Aunt Viv to send over one of her lawyers to represent him. Hopefully, he can get released on bail."

"Oh my God. I told him not to go there."

"Yeah, well it's hard to talk E out of doing something he already has his mind set on. Another thing I know about my boy is that he doesn't do things without carefully thinking it through. So do you want to tell me why my boy beat your fiancé damn near half to death?" he asked as he stood against the dresser, looking down on me. He reminded me so much of his father as he stood there. It was almost a little intimidating

"That man was putting his hands on you, wasn't he?" he asked. I hesitated before answering him. I didn't want him to go back and tell my parents, because that would have been an even bigger situation. I stood up and closed the room door.

"Yes, he's been abusing me for some time now. Early this morning, I had Enzo bring me to the hotel to get my things. Jean Claude said that he was leaving last night and that he would leave my things at the hotel. I went there to get my things while Enzo waited in the car. When I got up to the room, Jean was there, and he did some things to me. I was able to get away, and I ran to the balcony and called for Enzo, but he didn't hear me until it was too late. Jean had thrown me over the balcony."

I started crying as the images of me being tossed over the balcony replayed in my head.

"I couldn't hold on any longer. Enzo got there just in time before I let go, Chi. I would've been dead if it wasn't for Enzo," I cried.

"Shit, Kay," he said, walking over to me and giving me a hug.

"Why didn't you tell us what he was doing to you? That shit would have never happened if you had just said something."

"I know. His family is really powerful back in Paris. I didn't want to start a war with the family. You know how our family is. I just wanted to keep everyone safe."

"Who supposed to protect you, Kaylee?"

I was about to answer when I felt someone tap my leg. I looked down, and it was Mya.

"You cry," her cute little voice said. I wiped my tears and bent down and grabbed her hand.

"You know what would make me feel better? A hug. Can I have a hug?" I asked her. She smiled and reached up to give me the tightest hug her little arms could give.

"She's so perfect, Chi."

"I know. She really is. She'll be staying here from now on, so you'll get your turn to babysit."

"I would love to babysit," I said. I loved kids. I couldn't wait to have some of my own one day. I was excited every time my parents brought home new babies. I went so long being raised as the only child that I was happy to finally have brothers and sisters to play with. I wanted them to keep having more after KJ, but my mom had had enough. I guess it was now up to me to start having some of my own.

There was a knock at the door, and the door came open. The menace entered the room.

"I heard my niecey poo was here," Ruby said as she walked up to her. I still had my arm wrapped around Mya.

"Aye, don't be trying to steal my niece. Get your own, Frenchy."

"Whatever, Chucky doll. I have to go get my man out of jail anyway. Thanks, Chi," I said, kissing him on the cheek and then kissing Mya on her head. I started heading out the door.

"What? I don't get a kiss?" Ruby asked.

"Nope, you might like it."

"Sorry, you're not my type."

"I'm everyone's type, love," I responded, blowing her a kiss before walking completely out the room. I said goodbye to my aunt and uncle before hopping in my mom's car and pulling off.

MALACHI

I was sitting downstairs with my pops while Dr. Barnes and my mom were upstairs with Mya. Dr. Barnes was giving Mya her examination while she was asleep. I preferred not to be there, so I sat downstairs with my father. My father grabbed me on the knee.

"She's going to be alright," he assured me. I nodded my head. I had my hands folded in front of me while my head rested on them. I silently prayed that my baby would be alright. She didn't deserve the treatment she received, but I was going to make sure she never experienced anything like that again.

I heard my mom and Dr. Barnes voice coming down the stairs. I jumped to my feet quickly and turned to the stairs.

"What's up?" I asked as they both touched the bottom step.

"She's good. There's no sign of sexual assault. Other than the fracture in her arm, she's good. Her bruises will heal. I would suggest that you take pictures of the injuries and get the authorities involved. Child abuse is a very serious. I wouldn't take this lightly if I was you guys," Dr. Barnes spoke.

"We won't. We'll handle it, Dr. Barnes. Thank you for coming," my mom said.

"Anytime. Don't forget to bring her back to me in two weeks for a checkup."

"Aight, good looking, doc," I said, giving him a hand shake before he left out of the house. After he was gone, I went upstairs to Mya's room to check on her before I retired to the guest house. I wanted to take her with me, but she was sleeping peacefully, so I left her.

I laid back on the bed and just looked up at the ceiling thinking. I removed my vibrating phone from my pocket and pressed ignore once I saw it was Genesis calling. I don't know what the hell this girl wanted. She had better be calling to tell me she had the money to pay for my shit.

I looked over at the clocked. It was eight. I wasn't really ready for bed. My mind was restless, and so was I. I picked my phone up and opened up the message thread for Rhyes. I hit her up to see what she was up to.

Me: Hey Sweetie

Rhyes: Hello Malachi. How's everything?

Me: They could be better. I'm just laying here thinking about you.

Rhyes: Really? Aren't I a lucky girl.

Me: I want to see you. Can we meet somewhere or I can come to you?

I sat there for a few, waiting on her to respond. I guess she had to think about it because ten minutes later, she replied back.

Rhyes: Can I come to you?

Me: Sure thing.

I sent her my address and jumped in the shower. When I got out of the shower, I started straightening up the house a little. The place was still a mess from Genesis's retarded ass. I still couldn't believe she wrecked my shit.

When I was done straightening up, I ordered some Portuguese food from Pollo Campero. When I was done, I laid on the couch and waited for her to let me know she was outside. I was playing Panda Pop when I heard a noise coming from outside. I got up off the couch and looked out the open window. I didn't see anything. It was a cool breeze coming through the window, so it was probably just something brushing up against the house.

I went and laid back on the couch and continued my game. I had tried calling Enzo, but his phone just went straight to voicemail. He should have been out by now. I heard from Aunt Viv, and she said he was released on bail. The pending charge against him was aggravated assault. I tried calling Kaylee as well, but she didn't answer either. I was going to call back when I received a call that the food was out front.

I left out the house, shutting the door behind me. I walked through the yard and around to the house where the delivery car was. I paid the guy, and as he was pulling off, I noticed headlights coming up the driveway. The car pulled up next to me and shut the engine. She stepped out the car.

"Is here alright?" Rhyes asked. She looked great. She didn't have any makeup. Her face was natural which I loved. Her hair was pulled to the back, and she rocked an Adidas knee length track suit.

"Yeah, here is fine," I replied with a smile. She walked up to me and stood to her tippy toes to give me a hug. It was like she knew I needed one.

"I needed that hug."

"I know. I have a sixth sense."

I waved her to follow me as we walked back through the yard toward the guest house.

"I knew Ms. Camilla was living large, but I never expected this large," she said. I laugh.

"Yeah, my mom and dad are pretty low key about their finances. Did you find the place alright?"

"I got a little thrown off by the path up here. It was like I was driving through an enchanted forest."

"That entrance is a little dramatic. It was made for my little sister."

"Ruby?" she inquired.

"Yes. You know her?"

She laughed.

"Do I? Your sister is a piece of work. She was there when your mom did my interview. She called me a knock off Tony Childs."

I busted out laughing because that sounded like something Ruby's ass would say. She was always calling someone a knock-off or a Great Value version.

"What's so funny?" she asked.

"My sister. That girl is a trip and blind as hell because anyone could see that Tony Childs is the knock off version of you," I flirted. She stopped walking.

"That's how you get all the ladies panties off, huh?"

"Nah. I'm just speaking the truth. You're way more beautiful."

We made it back to the house, and we walked through the open door. I could have sworn I closed the door. I guess the wind blew it open.

"Welcome to my living quarters, Ms. Rhyes. The living room TV is cracked, so we're going to go sit in the bedroom, watch some Netflix, and eat some food. You do eat Portuguese, right?"

"I love it."

"Good."

We walked into the bedroom where I had lit a few candles. I hoped she didn't get the wrong impression.

"So did you break your TV to get me into your bed?" she asked with a smirk on her face.

"Maybe," I answered.

"That's a little extreme. Don't you think?" she asked.

"Nothing's to extreme for you, girl. I thought about pushing you in the pool by mistake so that you would have to get naked."

She laughed.

"All you have to do is ask, love."

"That's good to know. Where's Roy?" I asked as I pointed for her to have a seat on the bed.

"My sister, Ryan, decided to come home earlier, so I asked her to sit with him until I got back," she responded.

"How's everything with your daughter?"

"Not great, but they will be. I needed to get my mind off things. I'm happy you agreed to come over. We're still on for our date. I just needed some good company tonight."

"I'm happy you thought of me."

I looked down at her and reached down to place a kiss on her lips.

"Thanks for coming."

I sat down on the bed and started making our plates. I couldn't wait to eat. My ass was starving. Seeing as though we both hadn't seen Wentworth, we decided to watch it. We finished eating our food so that we laid back on the bed with her head rested on my chest.

Wentworth was pretty good, at least the parts I wasn't falling asleep on. I was nodding off like I was a junky or some shit. I looked down at Rhyes, and she too had dozed off, so I just said fuck it. I pulled the covers over us, shut down the TV, and closed my eyes.

I wasn't sure how long I was sleeping, but I felt something hit the bed. I ignored it and closed my eyes again. Once again. I felt something hit my leg. I opened my eyes and sat up. The lights were off, so I couldn't see anything. Again, I closed my eyes, attempting to go back to sleep until I felt Rhyes jump up saying ouch. I sat up in the bed.

"What happened?" I asked.

"I don't know. Something just hit me in the head."

"Huh?" I asked, reaching over and cutting the lights on. There were sneakers scattering the bed. That's what had hit my leg.

"What the fuck?" I asked, getting out the bed and walking over to the closet where my sneakers should have been instead of on the bed. I opened the closet, and this dumb ass girl was kneeled down in the closet.

"Genesis, what the fuck are you doing in here?" I asked her, pulling her out the closet by her shirt.

"What you mean *what am I doing here*? What is she doing here?" she had the nerve to question.

"I invited her here. You need to get yo' ass up out of here before I drag you out. You already broke up my shit."

"Well that's what you get for breaking up with me for this bitch. What's your name? Rice, is it?" she asked.

"It's none of your business, Ms."

166

"None of my business? Bitch, you in my man's bed!" Genesis shouted, running over to the bed and jumping on Rhyes. Rhyes balled up immediately to protect herself from the blows the Genesis was throwing. I jumped on the bed and pulled Genesis off Rhyes. I dragged her through the house and tossed her out on the lawn as she kicked and screamed.

"Leave, Genesis, before I call the cops on your ass and let them arrest you for trespassing."

"No, I'm not going anywhere. Make that bitch leave," she cried.

"Why would I do that? I want her here. I don't want you here, near, nowhere around. Now get the fuck on."

"No!"

"It's fine. I'll leave," Rhyes said, walking up next to me and squeezing past me as she walked out the door.

"Rhyes, no. You don't have to leave," I told her.

"Look, Malachi. I like you and all, but I'm not beat for this shit here. I'm way too classy for this hood rat shit she's trying to pull."

"Hood rat? I got your hood rat," Genesis said, running up behind us. I turned around quickly and pushed her ass straight in the pool.

"Just stay, Rhyes. Let me get rid of her."

"You do that. Call me when you do," she said, walking away. I watched as she disappeared in the dark of the backyard.

"Fuck!" I shouted as I started walking back to the house. Genesis had managed to climb out the pool and was standing there, dripping wet. I took one look at her ass, picked her ass up, and tossed her into the middle of the pool this time. I knew she couldn't swim.

"Help!" she screamed before she went under the water. She popped back up and screamed again before sinking under again. I picked up the two arm floaties and threw them in the middle of the pool near her.

"Good luck," I said before I walked back into the house and made sure I locked the doors behind me. I sent Rhyes an apology text before I laid back down in the bed.

TWO WEEKS LATER

MALACHI

*A*fter the whole Genesis fiasco, I apologized to Rhyes for everything that happened. I didn't want her to feel like I came with a bunch of drama, because I didn't. I even let Rhyes meet Mya. Mya adored Rhyes and vice versa. I hadn't seen Princess in two weeks, but we spoke every day, and sometimes she hit me up on Face-Time, and we would sit and chat. I could honestly say I felt like I was torn between two great women, and if I had to choose one, I don't think I would be able to.

Rhyes and I had met up at Palisades Mall so that we could get dinner. We ended up at Dave & Buster's where we had a bomb ass night.

"You had fun?" I asked her as we walked through the mall. I draped my arm over shoulder.

"Yeah, I had fun kicking that ass," she responded.

"Baby, I'm a gentleman. I let you win because it was the right thing to do."

"What?" she asked, pushing me in the ribs.

"You were putting your all in that game. I beat you fair and square, boo."

"Nah, I really let you win. I didn't want to send you home crying."

She placed her hand up as if she was telling me to talk to the hand. I was looking at her when I heard someone scream which caused me to look. Princess came running toward me full speed and jumping in my arms. To say I was surprised was an understatement. I never expected her to be so far over this way. She lived at least an hour away from here.

Once she was safely in my arms, she grabbed my face and started kissing me. For a moment there, I forgot Rhyes was standing there. I broke the kiss.

"Hey, baby, I missed you," she said with the cutest most innocent smile on her face. I knew there was nothing innocent about what she just did. I know damn well she saw Rhyes. I laughed.

"What you doing around this way, girl?" I asked.

"I'm here with my girl. You know Palisades be having all the dope stores. What you doing here?" she asked. I still had her in my arms at this point. I heard Rhyes clear her throat which made me put Princess down to her feet.

"This is my friend, Rhyes. Rhyes, this is Princess."

They both just looked at each other, not saying a word.

"Friend, like high school friend or something?" Princess asked.

"No, she's my friend like you are my friend."

"Oh, so y'all ..." she said, making a circle with her two fingers and sticking her pointer finger from her other hand in and out of it. I laughed. I couldn't help it. Princess was funny as hell, and she was cute with it which made it hard to get mad at her.

"Nah, none of that."

"Is it really any of her business?" Rhyes questioned with her hand on her hip. I knew it was probably best to cut this shit short.

"Well he said friends like he and I, and our kind of friendship involves fucking."

"Whoa. Chill, P."

"You know what? This is the kind of mess I want no part of. I'm out," Rhyes said, preparing to walk away.

"Rhyes, just wait up, ma," I said, grabbing her arm to stop her, but she snatched away.

"No, Malachi. I'm not doing this," she said as she walked away. We drove our own cars here, so I just let her go. It was probably best I let her go rather than cause her to potentially embarrass herself. I wasn't sure what the deal was, seeing as though she and I were just friends like Princess and me. The only difference was that Princess and I actually fucked once, and I was definitely looking forward to a second time.

I watched as she disappeared in the crowd. I looked over at Princess who just stood there.

"See what yo' ass did," I said, picking her up and wrapping her legs around my waist.

"Sorry, not sorry. She's way too sensitive, baby, but she's cute."

"Yeah, whatever. I liked her."

"But I thought you liked me," she pouted.

"I do. I like both of y'all the same. Unfortunately, you're a bit more chilled than she is," I stated, walking over to the bench and sitting down with her on my lap.

"Oh well. Her loss. Now can I have you all to myself?" she asked.

"I don't know if you can handle having me all to yourself, baby,"

"Try me. I'm a big girl."

"You definitely are. What you doing tomorrow?" I asked her.

"I don't know. It depends on what you say next."

"My little sister having a graduation pool party. You wanna come through?"

"I would love to. I guess I better look for me a bathing suit while I'm here then."

"Or you can just come in your birthday suit," I suggested.

"Yeah, right. Your mom already thinks I'm a hoe. I don't want her to think I'm a skanky hoe," she said, making me laugh. I'm about to get up out of here. I want to see my daughter before she goes to sleep. Hit me later?"

"Sure will, baby. Kiss that beautiful little girl for me."

I grabbed her face and placed a kiss on her lips.

"Have a good night, beautiful. Get home safe, aight?"

"Sure thing," she said getting up off my lap and running off with her friend. Her friend wasn't that bad looking. I was going to make sure she brought her friend with her tomorrow. She was Jace's type.

KAYLEE

had been home for three weeks, but it felt like it had been a month. I'd been beaten, raped, and thrown over a balcony since I had been back, and the worst was yet to come until now. I sat on the side of the bathtub, waiting to see if that nauseous feeling had subsided. I was convinced that it was food poisoning, but in the back on my mind, I wondered if I could have been pregnant. I knew it was too soon to tell, and I also knew it was too soon to be Enzo's if I was pregnant.

I stood up from the bathtub, bent over the sink, and washed my face. I dried my face and walked out the bathroom toward my bedroom. Pryce had come back a few days ago. She wasn't too talkative about her experience in Africa... that's if her ass really went to Africa. Anybody would be gloating if they had just come back from Africa. She didn't even want to talk about it, nor did she have pictures.

"Hey, sis. You alright?" I asked her as I peeked into her bedroom. She was sitting on her bed with her phone in her hand. She had a look of concern on her face.

"Yeah, I'm good," she answered, faking a smile.

"You sure?"

She nodded her head up and down. I left out of the room and went to get dressed for Ruby's graduation. The only way I would believe that Ruby was graduating was if I saw it my damn self. That girl terrorized that school. I'm sure all the teachers were excited for the day Diavion Ruby Jones got the hell up out their school.

Enzo was back at home. He was going meet me at the pool party. He had been released from all charges after beating Jean Claude up because Jean Claude failed to show up to court. He had hopped on a plane back to Paris before court, so the charges were dropped.

I had decided on a coral pink H&M dress and some flats. I pressed my hair so that it laid down my back. I applied some lip gloss and went downstairs to meet my mother and father.

When I got down to the kitchen, I opened the refrigerator, got a water, and then sat down at the table.

"What's wrong with Pryce? She looks distraught."

"I don't know. She hasn't really said anything since she's been back. Maybe she saw something that has her traumatized. Maybe I should go talk to her," my mom suggested.

"I tried to talk to her but she didn't say much. Maybe she just needs some time to adjust back to reality."

"Yeah, maybe. You sure you alright? You look a little pale," my mom said.

"Really?" I stood up walked over to mirror that was located near the door. My mom was bugging. I looked good. This dress was fitting me perfectly. I brought this like four years ago. I couldn't believe that I could still fit some of my clothes I had in that closet for years.

"Y'all ready?" my dad asked, coming down the stairs and standing in front of me in the mirror.

"Hater," I said, walking back into the kitchen to grab my purse. We got out to the garage and started getting into my dad's Bentley.

"Can I drive?" I asked, placing my seatbelt on. My dad looked back at me and then turned up the music to Jay-Z's new album *4:44*. I sat back in the seat with my arms folded across my chest. No one believed that I could really drive.

WE GOT to the graduation just in time. If I was driving, we would have been here by now. Uncle Troy, Camilla, and Malachi were already seated and holding seats for us.

"What took y'all so long?" Aunt Camilla asked.

"Traffic," my dad responded.

"If he had just let me drive, we would have been here on time," I stated.

"Yeah, we would have been here alright. Dead."

"Whatever."

The graduation had started. They called the Principal to take the podium. She came up there, strutting in her five-inch heels. She looked familiar, but I couldn't remember where I had seen her from. The whole time she stood up there making a speech, I just kept staring at her. I couldn't place her face. I tried to forget it, but it wasn't happening.

My mom's cellphone started ringing. It didn't interrupt the ceremony. The Principal just kept on with her speech.

I looked down at my mom's phone that she had in her hand and saw that it was KJ calling her. It hit me like Ike did Tina in the limo. My brother was fucking the Principal. I was stunned. This bitch was bold to bring her ass up in my parents' house, knowing that she was the Principal of their kids' school, cradle robbing bitch.

"You alright?" my mom asked, shaking my leg, bringing me back to earth.

"Yeah, why?" I responded.

"You look like you just seen a ghost."

I didn't answer I just kept on staring at the stage. *I am damn sure looking at a ghost because that's exactly what she gon' be once my mom gets done with her.* I made a mental note to talk to KJ later and give him the option of telling our parents, or I was doing it for him. One way or another, they were about to shut this shit down. The cradle robber called Ruby up to the stage, and we all took a deep breath.

"Yurp! Class of 2017! Squad up."

"Squad up," the graduating class all responded.

"Oh lawd. I can't watch this," Aunt Camilla said, covering her eyes.

I laughed because I never expected anything less from Ruby's ass. She stood up at the podium, fumbling with the tassel that continued to get in her face.

"How the hell they expect me to make a speech with this cat toy in front of my face?" she asked, and the audience started laughing. I just shook my head.

"I know some of you may not have actually seen me in class this year, because quite frankly, I'm smarter than most of your teachers, so let me introduce myself. My name is Diavian Jones, the smartest, dopest, baddest chick that has ever graced these hallways, and I am Saddle River Prep's class of 2017 Valedictorian."

Once again, the class cheered her on.

"I'm sure some of you are expecting a cute, smart, charming girl like myself to give a savvy speech about how we should all go out and reach for the stars and be the change that we want to see in the world. I'll let Nina handle that for me, but what I will say is that I am shocked to be looking at some of you in the audience. I never expected to be standing here, representing a student body of one hundred forty-eight. I didn't even prepare a speech for this moment, because I thought it was a joke when Principal Skylar told me I was the Valedictorian. I actually laughed in her face. Even as the days 'til graduation numbered down, I still didn't take this serious until the moment I was called on to stage. I figured I would just wing it, shit. I mean shoo," she said, correcting herself. I could tell she was starting to take it serious now.

"I haven't even chosen a college yet. That's how unprepared for life I am. You know, I sit up here and joke and make light of the situation, but behind that, I'm scared just like a lot of you. We're going out into this real world where Donald Trump is the damn president, and the unknown is scary. The only advice I can give to my fellow classmates of 2017 is to be you. Be you in a world full of fakes. No matter what the situations is, be you, and be you to the best of your ability. Stand out in a crowd. Be noticed. I'm sure, like myself, a bunch of you were told by teachers, parents, and maybe some peers that you wouldn't make it to senior year, and you wouldn't walk across that stage and accept your High School diploma. I know I was. I want you all, the class of 2017, to turn around to the audience, to your parents, friends, and teachers, and say look at me now."

The entire class turned in their seat and some even stood up and shouted, "LOOK AT ME NOW!"

"We started from the bottom, and now we're here. We're not perfect. We made mistakes, but we're here. To you the class of 2017, I'm going to close this with some inspiring words from her majesty, Queen Beyoncé Giselle Knowles Carter. Who needs a degree when you're schoolin' life? There's not a real way to live this. Just remember to stay relentless. Don't stop running until it's finished. It's up to you. The rest is unwritten. Thank you."

"Whoa! That's my motherfucking baby," Uncle Troy said as he stood up and was the first one to start clapping. The audience followed along, giving Ruby a standing ovation. The whole family just sat there stunned that Ruby just delivered an inspiring speech, and for once, didn't cause havoc."

The graduation continued. The Salutatorian made her speech before the Principal came back on the mic and started calling the students one by one to accept their diploma. When they called Ruby's name to accept her diploma, we all yelled and screamed as loud as we could. When it was over, we all stood in the back of the auditorium and congratulated Ruby, giving her the balloons, flowers, and cards we all bought for her.

"Hello, everyone."

The Principal had the nerve to come over to us. She looked around the crowd and noticed me looking at her. I could tell she remembered me because she quickly looked away.

"I want to say that it was a pleasure having Diavion in SRP."

We all looked at her like *yeah right, bitch.*

"Ruby, that speech was something else. I never expected anything less from you. Take care, and good luck in the future," she said, walking away. Ruby gave her the middle finger once her back was turned, and Aunt Camilla smacked her hand down.

"Hold up. I'll be right back," Ruby said, running away from us and toward some dude with dreads that held some flowers and a teddy bear in one hand and balloons in another. I guess that was her boyfriend by the way she jumped in his arms.

"Who the hell is that?" Uncle Troy asked, looking over there with the scariest scowl on his face.

"I don't know," Malachi responded. They both started walking toward Ruby. I was almost scared for what was about to happen to this man.

LIL' RUBY

hen I saw Chop standing there, looking as good as he wanted to be, I couldn't help myself. I ran and jumped in his arms. I disregarded the fact that my family was standing like a few feet away from me.

"You came," I said as he put me back down to my feet.

"I told you if you're invited me, then I would be here. That was a dope speech. I almost didn't recognize you, Baby D."

"Shut up. I had to tap into my sensitive side for a minute, but she's back. Are those for me?" I asked, pointing to the flowers, teddy bear, and balloons in his hand.

"Yes, they are. You like 'em?"

"They're beautiful."

"I also have this for you," he said, pulling out a box before he was interrupted by the goons.

"Yo," I heard Malachi call from behind me. I turned and looked at him.

"What, ugly?" I asked.

"Who's your friend?" my dad followed.

"This is Chop. Chop, this is my brother, Malachi and my dad, Troy."

I went around introducing everyone to Chop.

"How y'all doing?"

"We cool. Who you?" my dad asked like I didn't just introduce him to them all.

"I'm Chop, sir."

"I know who you are, but who are you?"

"Dad, this is my friend. Stop tripping, old man."

"What's in that box?" my dad inquired.

"He was about to show me until you came over here blocking. Dang," I said, turning back toward Chop.

"What's in the box?" I asked joyfully. He handed me the box, and I rushed to open it. It was a Pandora box. Inside was a Pandora bracelet with charms of a graduation cap, a 2017 charm, and a charm of the letter D.

"Aww, this is nice," I said, reaching up and giving him a hug.

"Your father bought me something similar for my college graduation, and I still have it. What was that, like eighteen years ago? Damn, we getting old, baby," my mom said.

"Yo, my man, how old are you?" Malachi asked.

"Chill, bro. Enough with the questions. Now can we go before I'm late to my own party? I'll meet y'all by the car," I said, grabbing Chop's arm and walking in the opposite direction. I could feel eyes on us as we walked, but I paid no mind to my crazy family.

"You're coming, right?" I asked him, trying to make sure he was going to be there so that he could see me in my new Fuck Me Bikini.

"I told you that if I'm invited, I'm there. I have to make a run real quick, but I'll be there as soon as I'm done."

"Alright. You still have the address, right?" I asked him.

"Yes."

"Good, so I guess I'll see you there. And I apologize for my family and their many questions. They're not used to seeing me with male friends. I told you that they thought I was a lesbian."

He laughed.

"It's cool, ma. I don't usually take too well to being questioned, but

I understand. My daughter better not ever think about introducing me to no nigga. I might dead his ass right there."

"So I'll see you in a few?"

"You sure will, beautiful. Oh, I have something else for you," he said, grabbing my hand and walking me toward his car. He reached in the backseat and pulled out a red box, something similar to the boxes you get from Edible Arrangements.

"I didn't want to give it to you in front of your family," he said, handing me the box.

"You didn't want to give me a box of chocolate in front of my family?" I asked Chop as I started opening the box.

"It's not just any chocolate, Baby D."

I continued to open up the box.

"Brownies!" I shouted with excitement.

"I'm about to get turned up."

"Take ya time, baby … a little at a time. I don't need you ODing on brownies, getting chocolate wasted and shit. Ya pops and brother already looking like they wanna kill my ass."

"Ignore them. Thank you for all of my gifts."

"You're welcome, baby. See you later," he said, placing a kiss on my forehead.

I said goodbye to him and walked back over to my family.

"You tell that nigga he put his lips on you again, I'm cutting them shits off and feeding them to your mother's dogs."

"Eww. Dad, stop being so overprotective. I'm eighteen. Come on, y'all. We left Jace, Nico, and Mega in charge. It's probably a bunch of naked stripper skanks inside of the pool by now."

"Ah shit. I didn't think about that. Let's go," my mom said, hurrying everyone along.

Pryce

I stood in my window with my phone in my hand with it on speaker. I had gotten back two days ago. Since I had been back, I hadn't heard from Kevin. I had been calling continuously, but he hadn't been answering his phone. Something wasn't right. He always answered my text messages at least.

I'd been sheltered in my room for days and didn't come out unless I had to use the bathroom or to eat. My family had been asking me questions about Africa, but I had been giving them vague answers because I didn't have much to tell them, being that I didn't really go there. When I got around my parents, I would put on a fake like I was all good. I think the only one who was suspicious of me was Bryce, and that was because we were twins and psychologically connected somehow. He always knew when something was wrong with me and vice versa.

"Shit. I mean shoo," I said, correcting myself.

"Why isn't he answering the freaking phone?" I asked out loud.

"Who?"

I turned, and KJ was standing at my door. I had no idea he was still here.

"What you doing here? I thought you were at Ruby's graduation party?" I asked.

"I'm on my way there now. You going?" he asked.

"I don't know, yet."

"What you mean? It's gon' be so many half-naked girls there. You might even find a boyfriend."

"Nah, I'm good," I responded.

"You're such a stick, sis. My ride is outside. I'll see you if you come."

"Alright."

I walked back over to the window as I continued to call Kevin's phone. I looked outside and noticed the waiting Lexus. I'm guessing that was KJ's ride. It was probably one of his little high school groupies. Once again, the phone went to voicemail.

You know what? I was going to this party. I was not about to sit here and miss out on the fun. This was probably the first time in a long time that all of my siblings and cousins were here together. This was going to be fun. Besides, I knew Jo was going to be there. Maybe I could get the scoop on what the hell was going on with her father.

I ran over to my closet and removed both of my bathing suits that were hanging up in the closet. I decided to wear my mint green one piece that crisscrossed in the front and back. While inside the closet, I started changing into my bathing suit. I heard my phone ringing, so I raced over to it while my bathing suit was only half way on. I jumped on the bed, grabbing my phone. It was only my mom. I answered.

"Hey, ma," I greeted with a little disappointment in my voice.

"Hey, baby. Are you coming over to the pool party?"

"Yeah, I'm on my way now. Are there a lot of people there?"

"Seems like the whole student body and their parents are here. I was just calling to see if you were coming," she said.

"Yeah, I'll be there soon. Ma, do you see Jo there?" I asked.

"No, like I said its so many people here."

"Okay, I'll be there soon. Tell daddy to go save me a parking spot closer to the house."

"Alright, baby. See you soon."

I hung up the phone, finished putting on my bathing suit and grabbed my bag before I left out the house and hopped in my beautiful car.

"Mama missed you, baby," I said, rubbing the dashboard of my car. I turned on my LeCrae album and pulled out the driveway. On the drive there, every now and then I would pick up my phone and look to see if there were any messages or missed phone calls from Kevin, but there was only a message from my mom telling me to park next to Ruby's car on the front lawn. I was really becoming concerned and mad at the same time with Kevin not answering his phone. I thought about pulling up to his home and acting like I was looking for Jo, but I talked myself out of it.

Ten minutes later, I was pulling up to the party. The driveway had to run about 250 feet long, and there were cars parked alongside of the driveway all the way up to the house. My mom was not lying when she said everyone and their mama was here.

I pulled onto the front lawn next to Ruby's Honda. The music from the backyard was banging. There were a few people in the front but no one I knew. I grabbed my bag out of the car and started walking up the stairs and into the house. I was about to put the entry code in that only immediate family knew.

"Pryce."

I heard someone call my name. I turned around.

"Hey, Mrs. Jonas. What are you doing here?" I asked, faking a smile, but deep down, I really wanted to know what the hell she was doing here.

"I'm here to see you, Pryce," she responded.

"Here to see me? Why? Is everything okay?"

"No. No. Everything isn't okay, Pryce, but you knew that. Can you tell me where you were for these past few weeks?" she asked, causing my breath to get caught in my throat.

"I was on vacation visiting some family. Why do you ask?" I questioned.

"It just so happened you were on a vacation around the same time my husband went on some bogus church visit. Two days ago, he got back from this trip, but I'm sure you know that. While he was in the shower, I took a little glance into his cellular phone, and I found these," she said, throwing a bunch of papers that smacked me in the face before hitting the ground in front of me.

I looked down at the papers that were on the floor. I bent down and picked some of them up. There were text messages between me and Kevin as well as some pictures he had taken of me while we were in Houston. In one of the pictures, I had on a white lace negligee, and in another picture, I was just wrapped in sheets.

I stood there in shock as I continued to look through some of the papers. I couldn't believe he had even saved all of these message and pictures, let alone allowed his wife to get in his phone.

"Mrs. Jonas, I am so sorry you had to find out like this," I said, finally looking up at her. The vision before me almost made me wish that I hadn't looked up. It made me wish that I had never started messing with Kevin. Mrs. Jonas stood there with a small gun pointed at me. She had a blank look on her face as if nothing I could say would change her decision. I held up my hands and started backing away.

"Please, Mrs. Jonas, don't do this," I begged as a tear dropped from my eye.

"The both of you are an abomination. He's a rapist, and you're a little adulterous whore. I placed five bullets in this gun this morning. There's three left. Two of them already rest peacefully in my husband's body, and two of them are for you. You are a sinner before God, and you must pay."

I watched in slow motion as she moved her finger to the trigger. I turned and tried to run, but it seemed as if I was running in slow motion. Two shots were fired, and I felt the hot lead as it connected with my back, entered, and exited my body. I fell to the ground, unable to feel anything. I was numb and cold. I watched as my own blood pooled around me. I think I was dying. I take that back. I knew I was dying. My eyes slowly started to close as I heard another gun shot before the vision before me turned black.

To Be Continued....

If you're interested in reading about the parents of these characters, check out my five-star series, A New Jersey Love Story and Knight in Chrome Armor available on Amazon now!!

ABOUT THE AUTHOR

At twenty nine, Myiesha is a proud mother to a feisty four year old little girl and Author of twenty two published novels. Born and raised in Paterson, New Jersey, she graduated from the famous Eastside High School where she went on to study Criminal Justice with a focus on Juvenile Justice at Berkeley College. Reading has always been an outlet in her introverted world. Myiesha's favorite novel is Black Scarface written by Jimmy DaSaint and Freeway Rick Ross. Myiesha has always had a vivid imagination which helps her cook up original and creative story lines.

Her first novel, A New Jersey Love Story was published in 2015 under Royalty Publishing House. It's spin-off series Knight in Chrome Armor went on to topping the Amazon Bestseller's list in the Urban genre. Since then she has released numerous titles under both Royalty Publishing House and Leo Sullivan Presents.

Now signed under Major Key, Myiesha plans to continue dropping bangers that will keep the readers on the edge of their seats and coming back for more.

Join my Facebook readers group:
Author Myiesha
Follow me on Instagram at
_miss_mason

Be sure to LIKE our Major Key Publishing page on Facebook!

CPSIA information can be obtained
at www.ICGtesting.com
Printed in the USA
LVOW13s0755140718
583547LV00023BA/424/P

GW